Best Days Of Our Lives

By Lloyd Watson

Chapter 1.

Porky knew that struggle was futile, but to acquiesce completely was unthinkable. He knew exactly what was in store for him – they'd told him in no uncertain terms and described it in graphic detail over the past hour. Whispers in the silence of the night, haunting and growing in intensity as the allotted hour approached.

Porky had laid awake, sweating despite the coolness of the night. He hoped something, anything, would happen to stop the inevitable. He'd even prayed. He wondered how many young converts made promises to God in similar circumstances only for God to ignore every single one of them. Did He know the promises were not truly sincere? Did He enjoy the fun of seeing people suffer or were there times when He just turned a deaf ear to the pleas of the suffering? Or perhaps there was a greater good that was being served by the pain – that seemed the most popular cop-out. But maybe He just wasn't there at all.

Porky struggled anyway. Well, at least until even he realised it was no longer in his best interests. But at least he'd made his point. Struck a blow for the oppressed. Let them know he was no pushover. The trouble was Porky knew deep down that he was a pushover – he was just soft. Soft as shit – as he was often reminded. Which was why he found himself looking up at the faces of his tormentors, their faces twisted into sinister grins. He could not call it a look of hatred but then, despite the old saying, looks could not really kill.

He was lying face up, being carried head first down a flight of stone steps. As he looked back up the stairs, he could see more faces. No smiles this time but all part of the grotesque scene, nevertheless. These were faces which betrayed feelings of concern. These were the faces of people who were not brave enough to take part, but were too scared not to be involved. These were the 'There but for the grace of God with hearing difficulties' brigade. The silent majority whose mute support empowered the minority and urged them on to even more audacious deeds.

Porky could hear the sound of running water as his body levelled off when he got to the bottom of the stairs. The grins got broader. He began to struggle again. It was safe to struggle again now because if he did manage to free himself, he'd only fall about a foot on to the tiled floor. Earlier he'd risked falling on his back on the edges of the stone steps. That was an entirely different prospect.

It had only been two minutes since they'd grabbed him but it had all happened in slow motion until now which, when coupled with the interminable threats before the snatch, made it seem like it had been going on for hours. Now, the world seemed to shift up a gear and accelerated into fast forward with everything becoming a blur.

He heard the words: "Hope the temperature is to your liking."

Suddenly he was fighting for breath. The cold water took control of his lungs and forced them to reject any oxygen that he'd managed to get in there before he'd been plunged into the freezing water. His arms and legs flailed in the water as he involuntarily continued to breathe in despite the fact that his head was under water.

Porky's head came to the surface with a rush. He heard the sound of laughter disappearing into the distance. 'At least no-one had stayed to hold his head under,' he thought as he hauled himself out of the old 19th century enamel creation that served as a giant bath. It was much bigger than normal, modern baths and could be a haven of pleasure when filled with hot soapy water which took an age to pour. But it was so easily transformed into a watery torture chamber by lowering the temperature of the contents to near freezing.

His thick flannel pyjamas began to give up the gallons of water they seemed to have absorbed while he was in the bath. A large puddle began to grow around his feet as he stood shivering and dripping.

Now it was incumbent on him to get out of the bathroom unseen after cleaning up the mess. It was a mess of his making, after all, seemed to be the argument for why he was responsible for the clean-up. They'd only helped him take a late-night bath, they hadn't asked him to get out again so soon and make such a mess on the floor. All the arm and leg flailing hadn't helped, either. But above all he didn't want to be the cause of everyone getting into trouble for 'a bit of fun' – now did he?

Porky took off his pyjamas and stood there naked, alone in the giant bathroom, while he squeezed them out in the bath. Then he pulled the plug out of the bath and put his wet pyjamas back on, before mopping the floor with a couple of towels which had been left hanging in the communal bathroom. He hoped they belonged to some of the group who'd bundled him into the bath. No point asking God to make it so. He'd more chance of winning the lottery. Slowly he trudged back upstairs, leaving wet footprints on the stone steps he'd just been carried down.

Porky pushed open the door to the dormitory which he shared with his attackers. Slowly he padded his soggy way back to his bed. All he could hear were badly concealed sniggers under bedclothes. It was dark but the moon lit his path back to bed. He took off his pyjamas. A low wolf whistle rang round the room as his ordeal was watched by unseen eyes.

He looked down at his bed. It was no longer the pile of covers he'd left less than ten minutes earlier. The covers were now pulled up as if he had never been in bed. The sniggers grew louder. Porky sighed.

Porky had been here before. He knew the signs. They'd apple-pied his bed. 'He must find out the origin of that expression one day,' he thought. Now he was more concerned about the fact that someone had messed up his bed. If it had been done properly – and he had no reason to believe these experts in torment had failed in their expertise this time – the bottom sheet would have been doubled up and folded over the blankets along with the top sheet. The effect was to make the bed look normal when in fact the length had been halved.

Porky looked at the bed. His mind flashed through his options. None of them would solve his problem or change the circumstances in which he found himself. In fact, none of them was particularly attractive at all, but he was used to having his options restricted to only those that caused him the least embarrassment.

'Quick, think', he thought, 'he could not continue to stand there like a dick. It would only increase their anticipation of the treat in store and enhance their enjoyment of his predicament.'

Porky grabbed the top sheet and pulled all his bedcovers off on to the floor.

That was different," he thought. *'Most people tried to get in and then either had to get out again to make the bed or alternatively, they slept all night curled up in a ball pretending they weren't bothered or hadn't even noticed the apple pie because they always slept in such an unnatural and uncomfortable position.'*

He slowly and painstakingly began to make his bed, shaking the sheets first and smoothing them down, before replacing the blankets and tucking them in with the regulation hospital corners, they'd all been taught a year earlier when they all started at St Elizabeth's Grammar School for Boys.

Porky's tactic had caught the others unawares and had spoiled the impact of the prank but his face-saving was minor and short-lived. They were not going to let a little tactical manoeuvre spoil a good night's bullying. A cold bath followed by an apple pie was a double whammy – a rare treat on one night. They were usually served up separately not both to the same person in the same session. Porky was honoured although he didn't feel it.

"Thought you, of all people, would fancy a bit of pie after your bath, Porky," said a voice from the other side of the room.

Giggling swept around the dorm like a sound moving from speaker to speaker in a Mexican wave of torment.

"You're too kind Tottie," Porky replied sarcastically, as he climbed back into bed, hopeful the night's troubles were almost over. He'd be able to sleep now. Tomorrow was a full eight hours away. Porky sighed and curled into a ball.

Chapter 2.

Brian Tottingham walked towards his Mercedes convertible and clicked the remote control to unlock the doors. The indicators flashed, the door mechanism clicked and the interior lights came on. He climbed in and leaned back into the deep, leather seats. He smiled.

'Another good night,' he thought. 'One of the best.' He savoured the moment, taking the time to indulge himself by reviewing the night's entertainment as the memories flashed through his mind finding the correct drawer in his filing cabinet of experiences.

The evening had begun well. He'd chosen clothes he felt were both particularly appropriate and also ones in which he felt comfortable and enjoyed wearing. Those were the best outfits – ones that suited the occasion and were fun to wear. Cream chinos and a heavy brushed cotton Ralph Lauren shirt, with Gucci loafers.

He'd arrived at the town centre wine bar slightly earlier than he'd planned which was acceptable – being late was not. Being late could have forced him to abort his evening – most unacceptable. He used the extra five minutes to take in the bar.

It was already fairly busy with after-work drinkers. They would spend the next two or three hours getting louder and louder until they all went their separate ways only to meet up at the office again in the morning, eager to bitch behind each other's backs about what had been said the previous evening. Some of them would not go straight home, of course. Some would double back after saying their ostentatious goodbyes with obligatory hugs and kisses.

They'd meet their evening's lover at a pre-arranged spot and scuttle away to 'scuttle' the night away in a sweaty session of sex, away from the prying eyes and gossiping tongues of their colleagues. They all knew, of course, but no-one had actual proof, although that would not stop it featuring in the coffee machine post-mortem on the evening.

It was only a matter of time before they were captured by a mobile phone, locked in an unambiguous clinch, and the incriminating evidence was emailed to anyone who knew them, or stuck on the office noticeboard like a modern-day display of a captured scalp. Unless they tired of each other first and then they'd babble happily about the affair with anyone who would listen but its currency would be seriously devalued by then. Fortunately for them, the whole charade was kept in balance because everyone was too busy making sure their own liaisons were kept secret to spend too much time and effort hunting scalps. Too busy watching their own backs to inform on others making two backs.

Brian had ordered a Coke and sipped it slowly. Tonight was not a night for alcohol.

The door opened and in walked two attractive tall, blonde women, both late twenties or early thirties and smartly dressed. Professional women by their appearance, chatting to each other and confident in their manner. They walked straight up to the bar without looking around, as if they knew they were unlikely to meet anyone they knew.

Brian looked around. The door opened again and more after-workers laughed their way into the bar. The two blondes had been served. They picked up their glasses and walked to a table near Brian's, and sat down. The smaller, prettier of the two sat facing

Brian, while her companion sat with her back to him. Brian smiled and took another sip of his Coke. The women were deep in conversation and hardly looked away from each other for more than half an hour.

Realising their glasses were empty, the taller woman got up to get refills, leaving her friend to relax and take stock of the bar for the first time. She looked around absently, her eyes pausing slightly as she looked across at a group of particularly noisy bankers who were being especially raucous. But her feminine sweep did not linger long on the group who doubtless would have expected much more attention from such a good-looking woman if they had not been so absorbed in their own company to notice her existence.

Brian watched her eyes. She was about to look in his direction. He looked down at what remained of his drink and counted to five. Then, he abruptly looked up and stared directly at the woman. She was looking at him and appeared embarrassed to have been caught staring. She quickly looked away.

Brian kept looking, knowing she would look back. She did, like a criminal returning to the scene of her crime. She blushed at being caught again, and looked away, but not before Brian had smiled at her. She turned and began fumbling in her handbag, producing her mobile phone. She looked at it as if she'd heard it ring and was surprised it wasn't hers. The truth was she did not want to be caught looking at a man on his own in a place like this.

'Where was Sally?' she thought, as she replaced her phone but continued to rummage in her bag.

Sally returned with their wine and sat down, providing her friend with a welcome distraction and a smoke-screen from behind which she could snatch another quick glance at Brian. He was getting up to go to the bar. She continued to watch him, safe in the knowledge that she would not be caught again.

"Nice bum," said Sally, who'd turned to follow her friend's stare.

"That wasn't what I was looking at," replied the blonde.

"Yeh, right. You never look at men's bums, do you?"

"That's not what I meant. I mean I wasn't looking at his bum. I seem to know him from somewhere. Do you recognise him?"

"I'd remember that bum," said Sally sadly. "So, no. I'm afraid I've never had the pleasure. Nor do I recognise him." She turned back to face her friend, who was still watching Brian at the bar.

"Julie, it may be an arse to die for but don't think you're dumping me to bugger off with Mr Lauren there," said Sally.

"Sorry, Sal, it's just spooked me a bit, that's all."

Julie turned her attention back to Sally and took a longer sip of her wine than she'd intended only to end up in a fit of coughing and spluttering. She finally surfaced and, catching her breath, looked around the bar to see if people were looking at her. Brian was and he was smiling. Julie found herself smiling back.

"You'll do anything for attention, won't you," said Sally.

"Come on, drink up. We're going," said Julie.

"Why? We've just got another and we'll never get a table anywhere else at this time."

"Because otherwise I'm going to have to ask him who he is and if I really do know him because he's just smiled at me as if he knows me."

"It's more likely he smiled at you because he'd just watched you drown in your wine, or because he'd like to get to know you," said Sally grinning at her friend.

"Oh, shut up. That's all you think about since you broke up with Stephen," snapped Julie, but broke into a smile as she said it.

"Hi, sorry to interrupt you but I couldn't help notice you and I'm sure we've met before," said a man's voice.

The women looked up to see Brian standing there, looking very boyish and almost apologetic at breaking into their evening.

"My name is Brian," he said, holding out his hand towards Julie.

"Hi I'm Julie and this is my friend Sally," replied Julie with relief in her voice.

"Actually, I was looking at you and thinking the same, before I nearly choked to death, that is," she continued.

"But I can't quite place you, nor your name come to mention it."

"Do you have a brother called Montgomery, by any chance?" said Brian, "Montgomery Sandal".

Sally tried to stifle a giggle. She knew Julie's brother was called Monty and that it was short for Montgomery but hearing his full name still made her laugh, especially as she knew how much he hated it.

"Yes. Monty is my brother," replied Julie. "He's a pilot," she added and immediately wondered why she had. It must have been pride in her big brother's success.

"I know," said Brian. "I'm a pilot too and I remember him showing me your photo. How could I forget? In fact, he's always showing me your photo."

Julie felt herself begin to blush.

"Oh really?" she muttered, subconsciously brushing an imaginary hair away from her face and becoming acutely aware that Sally was openly smirking at her from across the table.

"But I know we've never met," said Brian, looking puzzled. "So how did you recognise me?"

Julie smiled, relieved that she was no longer blushing and that she had solved the mystery.

"That's because Monty seems to be into showing people's photos at the moment," she said.

"He emailed me a load of them the other day and you seemed to be on most of them, in fact, I think you were on all of them.

"Although looking at one or two of them I'm not sure you would want me to have seen you in those particular situations," she giggled.

It was Brian's turn to blush. He looked a little embarrassed and said: "Sorry, sometimes things get a little out of hand. A group of off-duty pilots can be very similar to a rugby club or a group of students at times. You know – work hard, play hard." He paused.

"Some of us do know when to stop though – try to stop things going too far," he added.

"I'm pleased to hear it," said Julie, with genuine warmth.

"Well good to meet the famous Julie Sandal in person after all this time," said Brian.

"You're every bit as beautiful as Monty said and even more attractive than any of your photos led me to believe."

Julie felt herself blushing again as a warm glow spread from her neck up to her face and began to burn fiercely.

"Well, it's been a pleasure," said Brian, with a small bow. "I'll leave you to enjoy your evening.

"Sorry to have disturbed your evening and hijacked your friend. Please forgive me," he said, turning to address Sally.

"My pleasure," she replied. "I dream of handsome men disturbing my evenings."

Brian smiled and began to turn away.

"Perhaps we could have a drink sometime," blurted Julie, immediately regretting the note of desperation which seemed to have crept into her voice.

"Sure, that would be fun," said Brian. He reached inside his pocket and produced a card.

"Here's my number, give me a call sometime," he said. "Perhaps when Monty gets back in town after his three weeks in South Africa."

"Yes sure," replied Julie, thinking an evening with her darling brother playing gooseberry was not what she had in mind. She'd have to make sure she called while Monty was still safely on safari at the other side of a world.

"Bye," said Brian.

"Bye," said the two women in stereo.

'Yes, it certainly had been a good evening,' thought Brian as he turned the ignition key and the Mercedes purred into life. He chuckled as he pulled out into the evening traffic and made his way home to sounds of the rock music on his stereo system.

Chapter 3.

Julie emerged from the relative tranquillity of the customs hall into the mayhem of the arrivals area at Heathrow's Terminal Five. She was frazzled. Her business trip had not been a disaster but it had certainly not been an unqualified success.

This morning she'd boarded a plane to Paris for a meeting at which she intended to close a deal worth close to a million pounds. She'd walked into the offices in Rue Houssman with her lucrative designs in her briefcase and a presentation on her MacBook Air. Within minutes she realised her company was still only one of the contenders for the contract, not the winner, as her boss had led her to believe.

Quickly she'd shifted into sales mode and began to promote her bid rather than appear as the victorious designer, magnanimous in her superiority by praising her opposition for pushing her company into such a tough fight and prompting them into producing some of their finest work and how she was sure they'd chosen the right company in the end.

She'd left the meeting an hour later, drained, and her mind swirling from all the thinking on her feet, but confident that her designs were still very much in the race, if not yet the front-runner.

Now, after a flight that was delayed for longer than the eventual flight actually lasted and her bag going missing in baggage reclaim, she was still cursing the check-in assistant who'd insisted she had to check in her bag rather than take it as carry-on.

She emerged, scanning the lines of waiting drivers with signs bearing the names of their intended pick-ups. Julie could not see

'Sandal' or 'Xanadu', the name of the company she worked for, on any of them.

'Oh, bloody great,' she thought. 'A perfect end to a perfect day.'

She dug in her bag for her mobile phone to try to find out where her driver was.

"Hi, so we meet again," said a man's voice behind her.

Julie turned to see Brian, dressed in his pilot's uniform, standing behind her, smiling.

"You OK? You look, well a little ruffled, if you don't mind me saying so," he said.

"Oh hi," Julie replied. "I've just had a shitty day and now my driver hasn't turned up."

"I could give you a lift, which way are you going? Into town?" said Brian, with genuine concern. "Drivers are always failing to turn up which is why I drive these days," he added.

"It's OK, I'm sure he'll be here somewhere," said Julie, calling up the cab company's number on her mobile.

"I don't want to take you out of your way," she continued. "You'll be wanting to get home yourself. Just returned from somewhere exotic, have you?"

Brian laughed. "Sunny Frankfurt, actually. It was like a half day for me so I'm very happy to take you wherever you'd like to go."

Julie spoke into her mobile. "Hello, Julie Sandal here. I have a car booked to meet me at Heathrow, Terminal Five and he doesn't seem to be here. Can you check for me, please?

"Yes, the flight is more than an hour late but I still need to be collected," she said, with growing exasperation.

"No, I most certainly did not cancel it," she added after a pause.

"Well did you get their name because it certainly wasn't me. Why would I cancel a car I knew I needed and then ring you to ask where it was?

"Well, I'm not 'some people'," she shouted. "And he's not here, right? In that case how long will it take for you to get a driver here?

"Forty minutes," she exploded. "That's ridiculous."

Brian looked at her and jangled his car keys.

"Really I don't mind," he mouthed.

"Forget it," said Julie into the phone. "Don't bother sending anyone if that's the best you can do. I'll make my own way home but you'd better tell your manager that I'll be ringing tomorrow to demand an official explanation and apology for this. And I want a refund for the cab fare I'm going to have to pay to get home."

Julie smiled and winked at Brian as she hung up.

"That will buy us a dinner to say thank you for your kind offer," she said, adding quickly, "That is if you'd like to have dinner with me sometime."

"I'd love to," replied Brian. "And really it's no problem to give you a lift. In fact, it would be a pleasure to have your company on the drive into town. You can tell me all the embarrassing stories about Montgomery's childhood so I have plenty of ammunition for when he gets back to work."

Julie laughed. "Oh, there are plenty of those."

The drive into London took less than an hour, during which time they did indeed talk about the Sandals' childhood, a privileged one in Buckinghamshire, as it turned out. They also talked about Julie, her work, her likes and dislikes and a number of other areas of her life she would not normally have gone into on only the

17

second meeting with a guy. 'But it was so easy to talk to Brian,' she thought. 'Careful girl, you're falling for him'.

Brian pulled up outside Julie's terraced house in Chiswick.

"Can I invite you in for a coffee?" asked Julie. No matter how often or how sincerely she said that it always sounded like 'Would you like sex?'

"Perhaps a quick one," replied Brian, which might have been the answer to either question.

They both knew they would end up in bed. The only question which remained was whether they would actually have the coffee first. They didn't. In fact, they were barely through her front door before they fell into an embrace which ended with the desperate undoing of buttons, unzipping of zips and tugging of underwear over intertwined limbs.

The sex was intense and passionate, leaving them both dozing contentedly in each other's arms.

"Do you have to leave?" asked Julie.

"Well, I have an early start tomorrow but I can stay a little longer," Brian replied. Julie nuzzled deeper into his chest.

"Good," she murmured.

"But if I've gone when you wake up, please don't think I've run out on you," he said. "I'll leave as quietly as I can and I'll ring you tomorrow evening because I'm flying to Tel Aviv so you won't be able to contact me all day."

"OK," Julie said. "I'll look forward to it." She kissed him tenderly on the lips.

'Jesus', she thought 'This is all very soon for the lovey-dovey intimate phase to kick in.' She fell asleep with a smile on her face and an even bigger smile in her heart.

Chapter 4.

Brian typed quickly and silently on the computer keyboard. He glanced at the illuminated display on his Rolex. It was only 4 am and still dark but he was used to working by the glow of a computer screen.

His fingers skipped across the keys. The programme on an external hard drive attached to the computer began its work. On the screen, files disappeared and email applications opened and closed.

Five minutes later, Brian ejected the drive and shut down the computer. He took a quick look round the room and picked up his bag.

As he passed the partially open bedroom door, he saw Julie still curled up, deeply asleep, dreaming of Mr Right and how much he looked like Brian. But Brian was already only a dream. He may have hammered another nail into the coffin of a young woman's fantasy about romantic bliss, but it wasn't the first and it wouldn't be the last. In fact, it wasn't much of a nail at all – 'more like a drawing pin', he thought as he closed her door quietly and let himself out into the cold, early morning air. She would get over the disappointment quickly enough.

More important, Brian had got what he wanted. Sex – of course - and it had been particularly good. Julie was very athletic and enthusiastic. But this had never been about the sex, and given the things he was leading up to, Julie had got away relatively lightly. Not that she'd ever appreciate that, but then that was probably just as well too. It had been another successful session for Brian –

although 'Brian' knew nothing about it - and a successful session was what mattered, in fact, that was all that ever really mattered.

Chapter 5.

Porky was sitting on his own in the corner of the day-room writing a letter home. He didn't spend all of his time alone. He did have some friends but none of them was in with the in-crowd, therefore none of them would stick with him come what may – as demonstrated during the cold bath incident, and many others.

Writing home was always difficult. How do you write about how much fun you're having when you're not? How do you sound genuinely happy when you're not? It had not got any easier as the weeks and months went by. Like everything else in life – especially Porky's – there were ways of coping, ways to get around the problem.

Porky had toyed with inventing a group of friends, but parental visits were fairly regular and so the chances of discovery were too high. Now he just described things that had actually happened – just not necessarily involving him. He was midway through a vivid description of a recent rugby match in which he'd beaten two tackles to score the winning try in the corner. That had actually happened, he'd seen it with his own eyes from the touchline.

The door opened and in burst a group of noisy second years – the year above Porky. They ignored him, which was fine by him, and set up a table to play cards.

Porky returned to his try-scoring run. The card game began. It was bridge, an unusual choice but the current favourite throughout Porky's house.

The door opened again. Porky looked up. It was Tottingham, Nicholson and Stevenson. They too burst in shouting and pushing each other but paused when they saw the 2nd years in their day room. The 2nd years had a day room at the other end of the house so they were not normally to be found in the 1st years' room.

The three 1st years looked around and saw Porky in the corner.

"Hiya Porky," said Tottingham, walking towards him with a grin starting to form on his face.

The 2nd years looked up from their game and smirked. 'Porky' was a relatively new name and still caused mild amusement when it was used, especially when someone answered to it.

"Hi," he said and made a point of returning to his letter.

"What're you doing?" said Stevenson.

'Peddling a unicycle while conjugating Latin verbs,' thought Porky but instead replied: "Just writing a letter."

"Gis a look," said Nicholson, snatching at the paper. Porky was too quick and picked it up out of his reach.

"Oh, come on," said Stevenson, "What is Mummy's little poppet writing about that could possibly be so interesting that he wants to keep it a secret?"

"Perhaps he's telling her how much he loves to keep clean," suggested Nicholson.

"Always taking the chance for a quick bath," added Tottingham, who was well-versed in 'stating the bleeding obvious'.

They laughed uproariously at that, causing the 2nd years to again break off from their game and start to pay attention to events in the corner.

"Maybe he's asking her to bake him a pie," Tottingham continued, warming to his theme and keen to keep the attention of the 2nd years who were now smirking, their game suspended in favour of the day room theatre being performed at least partly for their benefit. Tottingham loved an audience.

The three 1st years were surrounding him now and Porky knew that the 2nd years presence would ensure his torment continued a little longer. He'd gathered up his letter. There was no way they were going to get hold of that, not considering the lies it contained. He'd never hear the end of the rugby story if they ever read it.

"So, tell us what you're writing about then Porky," said Nicholson, a thick-set boy whose weight far outscored his IQ.

"Just the usual stuff," replied Porky. "The crap food, homework, how I'm looking forward to half term."

"Why don't you ask if we can come home with you at half term," said Tottingham, who decided a change of tack might be more productive. He'd also started flicking Porky's ears as he was standing immediately behind him and wanted to double the chances of a reaction. "We could all have some of your Mum's lemon meringue pie."

The others laughed as Tottingham continued to milk the pie joke way past the point of exhaustion.

'If Tottingham's humour was a cow it would be dry and emaciated the number of times it was milked,' thought Porky as he moved to avoid another flick to his right ear.

Stevenson made a grab for the letter which Porky was holding in front of him. He managed to grab it but Porky pulled back hard. The letter tore.

"Oh, look what you've done now Porky, you stupid prat. You've torn Mummy's letter. She'll be so pissed off," said Tottingham. The others roared with laughter.

The 2nd years were still watching with interest and amusement. Stevenson looked at the portion of the letter in his hand and began to read. Porky had been lucky. He'd only torn away the portion containing his address and opening line, which read: 'Hi Mum,

Thanks for your letter. Sorry I didn't write last week as I've had tons of homework and ……'

Stevenson read it aloud anyway and got as good a laugh from his audience as if it had read: 'My darling Mummy, I cry myself to sleep every night and long for your comforting hugs.'

The only difference was that the real letter would not haunt him forever which the other one would have done. However, they were going to get some mileage out of Porky's homework overload. 'A small price to pay", thought Porky.

Porky screwed up the rest of the letter into a ball and stood up.

"You can't go now," said Nicholson, pushing him back into his seat. "You have to stick your letter together again."

"Otherwise Mummy will never know how much homework you've had," added Tottingham. "Perhaps she'll think you've been kidnapped if you don't send her a letter every week. Or she'll worry you've drowned in the bath."

This was the funniest line yet as all three of them collapsed over the desks holding their stomachs as they roared with laughter. And when the laughs began to fade, they forced some more, giving Porky an opportunity to leave the room, clutching the remnants of his letter.

He sighed and headed for the toilet. He looked at his watch. He had twenty minutes to re-write his letter before tea. Then he'd have the pleasure of sharing a meal with his compatriots while listening to the fascinating narrative of the letter incident. It would be interesting to see how much elaboration they had managed to add in only twenty minutes.

Chapter 6.

Julie picked up the phone and dialled the number Brian had given her in the wine bar, a week earlier. A voice informed her that her call could not be connected and that she should try again later. She'd already been trying for hours and had got the same response.

'Perhaps he's flying,' she thought. It was the same thought she'd had every time she failed to connect.

It was now a full day after Brian had said he'd call, and 36 hours after Julie had got up to find he had indeed left without her seeing him.

She'd waited patiently all day because of the problem with Brian being in the air. The hours had crept past as she waited for 6 pm – a reasonable time for him to call, she thought, as the time in Israel was a couple of hours ahead of the UK.

In fact, she'd waited until 10 pm UK time - with the help of a bottle of wine, four packets of crisps and a bar of chocolate - before she called him. She'd been calling him every couple of hours ever since and had now increased the frequency to every 10 minutes. But it was always the same response.

She dialled again – the same reply. 'Perhaps he forgot his phone and it's lying there switched off in his apartment,' she thought. The idea consoled her for a while until she realised that he had been meant to ring her and that it was easy to borrow a mobile, to say nothing of using one of the old-fashioned pay phones that still scattered the globe.

A light flashed on a computer screen in a penthouse flat overlooking the Thames. The man at the keyboard used his mouse to click on the light. A number appeared on the screen and below it another number. The man smiled and shook his head. Eighteen calls to the same mobile in less than 24 hours and they were getting more frequent.

'Boy she is taking it hard,' he thought. It gave him no pleasure but it did not distress him either. It was a small price to pay to perfect his art. A necessary inconvenience in an otherwise mundane life to further his experience. The light flashed again, but this time he did not pay it any attention. He was too busy to be distracted by a lovestruck woman. She was history. He was about to go to work, for real. He had a job to do and it would soon require his full attention.

Chapter 7.

Terrence Nicholson got out of his car in the factory car park and waddled the short distance to the entrance. He was already slightly out of breath by the time he entered the factory and he still had to climb the stairs to his office which overlooked the shop floor.

He usually spoke to the workers ending their nightshift as he arrived at work, to give himself time to catch his breath. It was hardly a friendly chat, more like ritual ridicule which his workers either tolerated or left his employ. Industrial tribunals for constructive dismissal had never made an appearance in the dog-eat-dog world of Nicholson's Pies.

Terence had taken over running the company a couple of years ago after the death of his father, who had built up the business from the two butchers shops he, in turn, had inherited from Terence's grandfather.

Old man Nicholson had started from scratch and worked his fingers to the bone to establish a good business from nothing. He was proud of how his son, Terence's father, had built on that success. A number of sound business decisions had taken a couple of shops into a business which was one of the leaders in the pie producing industry, supplying a number of big high street names as well as numerous school canteens and hospitals.

Fortunately, Terence's grandfather and father were no longer around because they would be appalled at how rapidly their legacy was disappearing. Terence was not a businessman like his father, nor was he a grafter like his grandfather. Terence was an idiot. A label he was amply demonstrating now as he held his usual 'banter' with the night shift who were tired and already thinking of going home to bed.

"So, are you still seeing that girl from the chip shop, Wiggie?" he wheezed to a shaven-headed youth with a nose stud.

Terence did not wait for a reply, instead, he launched into his usual routine and sang: 'Don't Cry for Me Fish Shop Tina' to the music of the theme tune to 'Evita'. Andrew Lloyd Webber would have cried himself if he'd heard Terence's out-of-tune rendition.

After a quick verse of that, which brought a few half-hearted smiles, he'd moved a few more yards through the factory. Now he turned his attention to one of his new targets. He had only worked there for about a month but seemed a good worker. The man was an illegal immigrant. Terence liked to employ illegal immigrants – no records, no tax, low wages, no hassle – all bonuses as far as Terence could see, but then Terence was not renowned for his far-sightedness. Employing illegal immigrants was just one of Terence's 'brilliant' business decisions. Terence's eyesight did not extend to being able to see that his business was failing almost as fast as his marriage had done last year.

"So, Ivan, what's been so 'terrible' overnight? he said, stressing Ivan and Terrible because Terrance knew the long-haired worker came from Russia, or Ukraine, or was it Poland? Terence did not care as long as he did not have to pay him properly and the man did not cause any trouble.

"Nothing terrible happen, everything good, Mister Nicholson," he replied in a think Balkan accent because he was in fact from Albania. He was a good worker, quiet and well-behaved. The others hardly knew he was there, well not until Terence arrived to put him in the spotlight every morning.

"Hope you haven't impaled yourself on any of the machinery," said Terence, sticking doggedly to his theme, regardless of the lack of humour.

"Wouldn't want you 'Russian' off to hospital," Terence chortled. This was a new line. He'd just thought of it and he considered it little short of comic genius. Even though this was its first appearance, the workers knew it would now be making regular appearances in Terence's repertoire.

"I no hurt, Mr Nicholson, sir. I very careful," said the long-haired Albanian. "Thank you, sir," he added.

"Don't worry son, only pulling your leg," laughed Terence, even more amused that the immigrant had missed the humour. 'Too sophisticated for him,' he thought.

He genuinely liked the new recruit. If only all his workers were so polite and bloody grateful for a job. Terence had always thought he deserved more respect, more reverence, more bloody laughter at his jokes.

'They'd laughed at my dad's jokes and they weren't anywhere near as funny as mine,' he thought as he heaved his bulk up the open staircase that led to his office. He puffed his way to his large leather chair and slumped into it, exhausted from his exertion and his humour.

'Time for a coffee and a Danish,' he thought, straining forward to the intercom so he could share the thought with Donna, his long-suffering secretary.

"Donna, time for me brekkie, love," he puffed.

"On its way, Mr Nicholson," came the disembodied reply.

Terence slumped back in his chair and looked at the papers scattered all over his office. He'd get Donna to tidy up a bit after she brought him his coffee. That would also give him a chance to ogle her and perhaps he'd get the chance of a quick grope if she came within range.

When he was a little fitter, he'd had the energy to give chase but now he operated within a danger zone of arm's length from his chair, which made it all too easy for Donna to avoid his lecherous grasp. But Donna knew how to play the system. She often strayed just close enough to raise his hopes and very occasionally she hovered just long enough for him to make contact. Her reward for this flirtation was that she got to come and go as she liked and was often rewarded with some extra 'pocket money', as Terence called it, 'to treat herself'. It was a small price to pay considering there wasn't a cat in hell's chance she would ever let him go any further.

Terence wheezed. 'Perhaps he should cut down a little,' he thought. He was puffing a little more than usual. Even he had noticed it over the last couple of weeks.

He patted his pocket, looking for the blood pressure tablets the doctor had given him as he'd delivered his monthly warning about smoking, drinking, eating fatty foods and how he was killing himself.

'Bloody doctor' thought Terence, but he had cut down on all three and yet he was feeling worse than before.

Donna opened the door and walked in with his coffee and a Danish pastry.

"Here you go," she said, putting them on his desk, keeping her body safely out of range.

"Actually, I'll not bother with the Danish this morning, just the coffee," said Terence, still searching for the tablets.

"Are you OK?" asked Donna, incredulous that he was passing up the opportunity for food.

"Of course I am. I just don't fancy a bloody Danish," Terence snapped.

"I didn't mean that," replied Donna, "You just look, well you look awful."

"Oh thanks," said Terence. "I'm just a bit knackered this morning, that's all. Heavy night last night. Hardly got any sleep. You know how it is," he lied.

"Of course. No doubt you were getting plenty of exercise though," she said, winking.

Donna knew full well Terence was lying but it was all part of her adopted duties. She certainly wasn't going to let him even get close to her today, let alone touch her, so she thought the least she could do was humour him by playing along with his 'jack-the-lad' fantasies.

Terence had failed to find his tablets so he reached for a bottle he spotted on his desk. He poured a couple of tablets into his hand and swilled them down with a swig of the coffee.

"Donna love, this place could do with a tidy up when you've got a minute," said Terence. "But maybe give me ten minutes to finish my coffee and deal with the urgent mail. I'll buzz you when I'm through."

Donna nodded, knowing Terence would do absolutely nothing for an hour, which would give her loads of time to finish the crossword and ring her boyfriend.

She left Terence's office and walked along the open walkway back to her office. There was a couple of wolf whistles from the factory floor.

OK, she was pushing 40 and had seen better days, but Donna prided herself she could still turn a head or two in the far from competitive world of meat pie production. After all, she did not have to wear one of those silly hair nets the other women had to wear, nor a shapeless overall. Also, an overhead walkway was a God-send for attracting admiring glances, especially if your skirt was just a little too short for your age. Donna smiled at the attention.

The Albanian smiled too as he looked up at Donna and at the Danish pastry she was carrying in her hand. Then, he left the factory along with the rest of the night shift.

Chapter 8.

"It's weird. It's just as if he's disappeared," Julie was saying to Sally as they sat in the same wine bar where two weeks earlier, they had met Brian.

"In fact, it's as if he never even bloody existed," she added, taking a sip of her wine.

"Of course he existed. I saw him," said Sally, who had talked Julie through more than one failed relationship.

"I'm serious, Sal," said Julie.

"He's just found someone else and hasn't called, nor is he taking your calls," said Sally. "It's the age-old problem once they get what they want," she added.

Julie ignored the reference to her eagerness to consummate what had really been little more than a casual meeting.

"It's more than that," persisted Julie. "Ok, so he doesn't call. I can believe that. That always happens eventually," she added with an ironic smile. "But I've tried ringing him from a switchboard number and so he wouldn't know who was calling and he still doesn't pick up."

Sally just raised her eyebrows and waited for Julie to continue.

"Also, I emailed my brother in South Africa to ask about him and he's just replied," Julie continued, looking more serious.

"He doesn't know any Brian Tottingham, Sal. He doesn't work with anyone by that name. He said he can vaguely remember a younger boy at school being called Tottingham but he couldn't remember if he was called Brian. They all called him Tottingham and his friends called him Tottie."

"Really?" said Sally, getting a little more curious about her friend's failed love life. "Maybe you misheard the name."

Julie grunted dismissively. "Do me a favour I don't sleep with people and mishear their bloody names."

"Well not in this country anyway," said Sally.

Julie punched her across the table. "That's different," she said. Sal this is serious. It's spooky."

"Sorry, I couldn't resist that," Sally said apologetically.

"So have you rung the airport to ask for him in case Monty is winding you up?"

"Yep, I did that before I emailed Monty. That's partly why I emailed him at all because they denied he worked there and that was what got me thinking."

"But you met him at the airport after his flight from Rome, or wherever it was," said Sally.

"Frankfurt," corrected Julie. "I know I did, but I suppose I never saw him get off a plane. And that's another thing. My taxi was cancelled. Thirty minutes earlier, someone – a man – rang my cab company and cancelled the booking for my pickup. Quoted the right bloody number and everything."

"You don't think that was him, do you? Don't you think you're becoming a little paranoid about this? There must be a simpler explanation."

"Well, you explain it then," said Julie. "Can you make it make any more sense. I've thought it through a thousand times and it just doesn't add up."

"What about those pictures you had of him and Monty? He must know him," remembered Sally.

"Ugh Ugh," said Julie, shaking her head. "That's what I thought too but they're gone."

"What do you mean, gone?"

"I mean, gone, not bloody there, disappeared. What do you think I mean?" said Julie with exasperation in her voice.

"Where were they?" asked her friend.

"Monty emailed them to me so they were on my computer, attachments to his emails. Now they're not there."

"Did you ask Monty about the photos?" said Sally, beginning to share her friend's concern.

"Yes, I did. He denies sending any photos of that guy. He said he sent some photos which had work colleagues on them. Nobody called Tottingham. Nobody who even remotely looked like my description of him."

Sally looked blankly at her friend and took a sip of wine because she could not think of anything sensible to say.

"I asked Monty to resend the photos so I could identify the bastard," said Julie, after the pair had sat in silence for a couple of minutes.

"But when the photos came none of them showed the guy I swear was in them the first time. It's as if he was never there. God, I wish I could meet him again if only to give him a piece of my mind for pissing me about," she went on with more strength in her voice than she really felt because the whole episode had actually shaken her up more than she wanted to admit. A lot more than she would have expected. But it was all just so weird.

"Don't give him too much of your mind, you've barely enough to function as a life-form as it is," said Sally, sensing Julie needed a distraction from the seriousness of the situation.

"I knew I could rely on you for your support in time of need, you cow," replied Julie. "Come on drink up, let's have another." And she bounded to her feet with forced enthusiasm.

"Oops sorry," she said, as she bumped into a long-haired man who was making his way to the door.

"It no problem. It my fault. Really. Sorry. Please," said the Albanian. That was the closest Julie would ever get to meeting 'Brian' again or to an apology for all she'd been through.

Chapter 9.

Lemure checked his personal emails. He didn't get any spam mail due to the heavy layers of encryption and the numerous filters he had in place. It did not take him long, he received very little personal email of any sort.

Checking his mail was a daily ritual which he performed whatever his other duties or wherever he was in the world. Lemure liked to be on top of developments. He hated surprises. He always had done.

He tapped a couple of keys and switched email accounts. A series of folders appeared on the screen before him. He checked each folder thoroughly, pausing only to transfer copies of some emails into different, named folders, adding notes here and there.

His main task today was to tidy up after his latest training exercise. He'd already wiped Julie's computer of any trace of emails or photos relating to him. He was now deleting the photoshopped photos of her brother into which he'd inserted his photo before she'd looked at them. Once he was happy there was no trace of his existence in her life or that of her brother, he switched to another folder. He saw her brother had resent the photos - which obviously didn't include him - but that was fine. It would just add to the confusion and mystery.

Lemure lived alone, had done for almost ten years since his wife Diana moved out. Not that he'd given her much choice after he discovered she was seeing someone else. He didn't even wait to find out how serious the relationship was. To Lemure, it was an irrevocable breach of trust and to him, that was a black and white issue so it would serve no purpose to discover where the affair sat on the sliding scale of adultery. To him, flirty emails and after-work meetings were the same as rampant sex in the stationery cupboard. He could not bear to be let down after he'd put his trust in someone.

Still, she was gone now, leaving Lemure to get on with his life in the sort of efficient and methodical way he would have lived it all his life if he hadn't got married. It also enabled him to disappear from his previous existence altogether and to be reborn as Lemure, a man without ties, without a history and without obligations.

His apartment was sparingly but tastefully decorated and he'd got rid of anything from his life that was not functional. Anything of sentimental value had gone too. He believed in not surrounding himself with things he could never leave behind.

After his marriage broke-up he found it surprisingly easy to avoid becoming attached to anyone, or anything. But at the moment he wasn't at home. He was using a rented apartment and that was not exactly decorated to his taste. But it was functional, served his purpose, was in the right area and most importantly, it was untraceable.

He sat back from the computer screen and picked up the remote for his stereo unit. The apartment resounded to the music of the Foo Fighters. Lemure closed his eyes and tried to focus on what he needed to do before he grabbed some sleep.

Everything in Lemure's life happened because he wanted it too. It had not always been that way. He'd always tried to be organised and on top of things, but since his ex-wife had gone, he'd removed any element of love from his life. There was no way he'd be caught out and humiliated again, although he had to admit it was a shame his present lifestyle prevented him from having a dog again.

He opened his eyes and began to type at his keyboard. Columns of figures appeared and Lemure began to study them intently.

Chapter 10.

Porky sat down for lunch. It had been a good morning - all things considered. Any fun – or bullying depending on your perspective – had been aimed elsewhere, leaving Porky free to enjoy the anonymity which had become so appealing to him recently.

He didn't like to see others being picked on, and there was always a slight feeling of guilt as he stood by and did nothing to help, but the sense of relief that it wasn't him was so overwhelming that he could not help savouring the moment.

It was Friday so it would be fish and chips. Equality of portions was his only problem now but this week his table was playing host to the Head of House, a sixth former who was well respected by teachers and boys alike. Steve Howie was very fair. He'd also seen most of it before as he'd grown up through the various school years. He'd see to it that everyone got an equal share of chips – the most coveted of all food. He'd also moved Nicholson and Tottingham up the table to sit on either side of him so he could keep a better eye on both their behaviour and Nicholson's voracious appetite.

Porky allowed himself a little inner smile. 'Not a bad day at all and his favourite meal,' he thought.

True enough, just as Porky had expected, Nicholson and Tottingham were kept well in check, and Stevenson, separated from his cronies, was left floundering like a fish out of water at the other end of the table.

'Nice move, Howie,' thought Porky. 'He'd be a captain of industry one day or a general in the army, with those natural man-management skills.'

The plates all collected and taken away, two servers from each table were dispatched to collect dessert from the central serving hatch. They returned less than a minute later with a pile of plates and a large metal dish.

Porky inwardly groaned when he saw the dish, covered in a sea of white foam. And just when his day had been going so well. Tottingham and Nicholson saw the dish's contents at the same time and their eyes lit up.

"Mmm lemon meringue pie, yummy," said Tottingham, licking his lips in exaggerated anticipation of the dessert – and the fun that would accompany it.

"It's Porky's favourite, isn't it, Porky?" he added.

"Is that right, Pye?" said Howie, oblivious to the undercurrent in the conversation and taking Tottingham's words at face value – always a mistake in Porky's book.

"Yes, I do like it", replied Porky truthfully, but knowing he was just letting himself in for a longer conversation about the dessert than might have been the case if he'd lied and said: "No".

"Yes, we all love lemon meringue," said Nicholson.

"Is there anything you don't like Nicho?" said Howie, dividing the pie up into 10 equal portions. Everyone laughed. Nicholson grinned.

"I don't like cough medicine," he replied after a moment or two racking his brains for something he didn't like.

"Well just as well we rarely get that at meal times, isn't it Nicho?" said Howie, raising his eyebrows to the others at Nicholson's stupidity.

"But I'll certainly tell cook to make sure she doesn't put any in the gravy anymore, now that I know you don't like it," he added,

"Oh cheers, Howie," replied Nicholson, genuinely pleased that the Head of House was personally going to intervene to ensure his one hate was now going to be removed from his diet altogether.

"You dick, Nicho," said Tottingham, kicking him under the table. "He's joking."

"I know, you spaz," replied Nicho instinctively, but Porky could tell he was lying and also that he was hurt by Tottingham's open rebuke. That didn't happen often but the opportunity to show off to Howie was too tempting for Tottingham, even if it did mean rounding on one of his most loyal cronies.

"OK you two, that's enough," intervened Howie, restoring order to the table, which was falling about with laughter and drawing curious looks from the other nearby tables.

"Settle down and eat," said Howie. The laughter subsided and the boys began to pass plate after plate down each side of the table as Howie served out the portions.

Porky began to think the worst was over but he should have known Nicholson would be anxious to restore his credibility before the end of the meal.

"Has lemon meringue always been your favourite, Porky?" he said.

'Oh, here we go,' thought Porky. "I've always liked it," he muttered noncommittally.

"I think it's my favourite pie too," Nicholson continued.

"Yes, mine too," added Tottingham. Nicholson smiled, pleased that he was back on side with Tottingham.

"Although I like all pies really," Tottingham continued. Howie raised his eyebrows and kept eating. Sometimes he despaired at the level of conversation on the junior tables. It was a much more entertaining affair when he sat on one of the senior tables. He could join in the conversations and didn't have to act as a meal referee.

"You enjoying it Porky?" said Stevenson from the other end of the table, keen not to be left out of the fun now that it was hotting up.

"Mm," muttered Porky. Then it happened. Nicholson leaned over to get the water jug and knocked a water glass over. Most of the water splashed onto Porky's plate, the rest spilt on to the table and ran off into his lap, despite his attempt to spring to his feet as soon as he saw it happen. He was too late. There was a dark stain on the front of his grey trousers.

"He's pissed himself," said Stevenson, predictably.

"Shut up Stevenson," said Howie. "Nicholson, you clumsy oaf. Go and get a cloth."

"Pye, go and try to dry your trousers before afternoon school," said Howie, turning his attention to the soggy schoolboy.

"If you don't get them dry go and see Matron to borrow a spare pair. We can't have you going into school looking like that."

Tottingham sniggered. "We don't want people thinking that Aston boys wet themselves do we Howie?" he said.

"Shut up Tottingham. You are not helping," Howie responded.

Nicholson returned with a cloth and began mopping the table, a broad grin across his pudgy face.

"Don't you want the rest of your lemon meringue, Porky?" he shouted across the hall as Porky opened the door to leave. He could feel the eyes of a hundred boys burning into his back. He did not reply, nor even turn round, but he could feel the familiar sensation of tears welling up in his eyes.

'Thank goodness he was facing away from the dining room and would have time to compose himself again before anyone would see him' he thought.

"Shut up Nicholson, you can clear the whole table for making such a mess," he heard Howie say as he left the room.

"And if I thought you'd done that on purpose you'd be spending an hour after school writing lines."

Porky had no doubt Nicholson had done it on purpose. It had happened before, but not when Howie was chairing the table and so he had not made the connection. Nor did he know the derivation of Porky's name. Therefore, he had not appreciated the undercurrents that had led up to Nicholson's bout of clumsiness. Howie just assumed it was another stupid childish nickname which boarding schools seemed to churn out by the day. Of course, it was just as childish and stupid as all the others but knowing where it came from might have enabled someone like Howie to see through the build-up to the 'accident'.

Porky's real name was Nigel Pye. It didn't take long for the collective imagination to start playing with the word 'pie' to create a nickname. For a while he got called most of the fruits that could be cooked in pastry. But it was only when Porky's tormenters moved on to varieties of meat pie that they particularly liked 'Pork Pie'. From there, it was such a small, and eminently logical step for a 12-year-old brain to get from 'pork pie' to 'porky pie' and so was born the lasting nickname of 'Porky'. Pies remained an easy 'in' to goad Porky.

That was why Porky had no doubt the whole charade was an elaborate stunt, but if enough 'evidence' pointed in a certain direction, it was amazing how most people assumed that must be the right direction.

He'd known something would happen the moment that pudding had arrived and they'd made the inevitable connection. Now he had 20 minutes to get his trousers dry. The thought of going back into school with a 'piss patch' was too awful to contemplate. But then going to school in a pair of borrowed trousers was even worse. They would not fit him properly and one of his fellow diners would make sure all his classmates knew Porky was in someone else's trousers.

Porky shuddered at the thought and at the numerous causes of amusement that would appear with that revelation. He gritted his teeth and scrubbed his trousers even harder with the towel.

Chapter 11.

Terence was sweating heavily, but it had nothing to do with exhaustion, or the heat. This was stress. He'd just spent an extremely uncomfortable 30 minutes with his accountant, and it wasn't over yet.

Within minutes of the meeting starting, Terence realised this was not going to be like any other meeting he'd had with his accountant before, and he'd had plenty of uncomfortable sessions with his accountant. He'd told him things weren't going well but he'd always been confident that with a bit of fiddling here, or a bit of sharp practice there, he'd be able to delay what seemed inevitable to everyone but Terence. His own idleness and ineptitude were slowly killing off his family inheritance. The pace of the demise seemed to have picked up in recent months and now, it seemed the bean-counter was here to administer the last rites. The word 'receivership' had been mentioned in the opening sentence of the meeting. That hadn't happened before.

"......... a very slim chance but it might not work," the accountant was saying as Terence again tuned into what was being said. He was still struggling to come to terms with the fact that his golden nest egg was tarnished beyond repair, and it was starting to dawn on him that it was all his fault. The golden goose that laid it had died along with his father. All Terence could ever have been expected to do was keep the egg polished by keeping things going. He'd failed spectacularly.

"......... cutting right back to the core business which will mean layoffs – lots of them," the accountant was saying.

"But that means lots of money in redundancy pay-offs," he continued.

Terence saw a glimmer of hope. He didn't give a damn about job cuts if it meant he could continue to avoid real work himself.

"What if the redundancy pay-offs were not as much as you might expect?" he asked. It was the first time he'd spoken for 10 minutes.

"What do you mean 'not as much'? asked his accountant. "You have to pay the statutory minimum at the very least, or you're in big trouble."

"I mean what if we didn't employ as many people as you might think?" said Terence.

"Explain," sighed the accountant.

Tony Rosling had been the family accountant for years but he'd already come to terms with the fact that the company was no longer run along the same lines as in previous generations. He'd already turned a blind eye to a number of irregularities, although nothing that he thought would ever be discovered and reflect on him. But he wasn't sure what foul-smelling rabbit Terence was going to pull out of the hat this time.

"Well let's just say that some of our workers are not necessarily entitled to full statutory pay-outs," Terence replied. "Some don't even work here at all."

"How many illegal workers do you have Terence?" said Rosling, impatiently.

"Just one or two," smiled Terence. "But would that make a difference to the pay-outs?"

"It might," answered Rosling cautiously. "But only if there were more than one or two."

"Well, there could be a few more."

"How many?"

"Not sure exactly but possibly, say, more than half of them."

"More than half of them," repeated Rowling. "Jesus, you'll never get away with that. They are bound to go running to the press, or the unions, or even the police."

"I don't think so," said Terence. "You see it's not only a job to them. Most of them would find themselves back in their beloved homelands if they draw attention to themselves and I don't think they'd want that. No, I think you'll find they'll just pocket an extra week's wages and move on to the next illegal job."

He smiled a pudgy smile for the first time since Tony Rosling had entered his office.

Rosling frowned and said: "Well that might help a little but it will only delay the inevitable a little longer unless you make a serious effort to turn this company around. Go back to the basics that put the company where it used to be," he continued, adopting the lecturing role he'd taken up after the death of Terence's father.

Someone had to talk some sense into the oaf and Rosling didn't know anyone still involved with the firm, or even anyone still in Terence's life, who was remotely qualified for the role, other than him.

"One more problem, one more major cancellation, or anything which endangers the business and it's over Terence. Believe me, it really is over. Now get rid of those extra workers and sort this business out," he added as he got up to leave.

"And don't leave any trace or tell me how you do it. I know nothing about those workers or the terms on which they are employed," he added.

But Terence had already switched off and was thinking of what he was going to have for lunch. The immediate crisis seemed to be over and it would only take him sacking a few foreigners. Terence wished everything was as simple. He was sitting back in his chair smiling as the door shut behind the departing accountant.

Lemure switched off the receiver and he too sat back smiling.

'So, the end is nigh' he thought. In fact, very nigh. It would have to be tonight. Terence may actually act as swiftly as he needed to on this occasion seeing as it did not involve any real work. Just a load of letters which Donna would have to type and then hand out to the workers, and it may not even involve that much administration if Terence wanted to reduce the paper trail even further. It might happen as soon as tomorrow, although Lemure doubted even this crisis would provoke Terence into such a speedy response.

Still, he would take no chances. Lemure never took chances.

Chapter 12.

The Albanian walked back home from the bus stop. He'd had a good night's work – one of the best. It was also his last, well his last night at Nicholson's Pies, at any rate. He'd been sacked as he finished his night shift. Donna had walked around and given out envelopes to most of the night shift. A couple of old timers had been spared, probably because they were the only legal employees. Anyone who queried the payoff was simply told 'last in-first out'.

The Albanian hadn't queried anything. He hadn't even opened the envelope to see how much money he'd got. It wasn't important. He would no longer have to watch that fat pig strut through the factory being rude to people who were not in a position to tell him what they really thought of him, or where he could shove his job. Lord knows there would have been plenty of room in there!

The shift had begun well, as there were a number of people who had phoned in sick and no-one really seemed in the mood for work. People spent the first two hours looking for reasons not to work – toilet breaks, cigarette breaks and chats in the corner near the coffee machine. Even the shift supervisors seemed happy to look the other way.

Not wanting to be left out, the Albanian had made good use of his time away from the production line. He'd paid a visit to the 'grand sty in the sky' – as Terence's office was known to the workforce. He'd only been in there a couple of minutes but it was long enough as he didn't have much to do.

Then, midway through the shift when everyone else took a meal break, the Albanian had opted to stay on the line and eat his sandwiches on a bench at the back of the factory floor.

For five minutes he'd been totally alone while the machinery continued to produce pies and other meat products, which was a clear breach of Health and Safety regulations, but they were never a high priority at Nicholson's Pies. Only the packers stayed at their positions but they were through another door.

Again, five minutes was easily enough time for the Albanian to empty the contents of a phial into the food mix. The chemical was quickly churned into the other unspeakable ingredients that went to make up Nicholson's Pies.

'Not a bad night's work at all,' he thought, as he walked into his temporary home and took off the long blond wig.

Thank God he didn't have to wear that again for a while. And no more of those hideously disruptive night shifts, to say nothing of an end to the foul smell that filled his nostrils and seemed to stay with him until his next shift.

Lemure slumped into a chair. He needed a shower. No, he needed a bath. He needed to soak in something scented to remove the taint of Nicholson's Pies.

Lemure closed his eyes and wondered how long it would be for the 'proverbial' to hit the fan.

'A couple of days at most,' he thought. The pies would be delivered throughout today and be on the shelves tonight, or tomorrow, depending on the distance. They should be on sale for a maximum of a couple of days.

So, by the weekend, there should be news of a nasty case of food poisoning which would fairly quickly be traced back to Terence's factory.

By the time the environmental health people traced the source and closed down the premises for examination, poor old Terence would have no way of even tracing 80 per cent of the people working on the shift that had produced the bad batch - because he'd just sacked them all. Nor would there be any trace of the listening equipment that had been fitted in Terence's office for the last few weeks.

Lemure smiled at the memory of some of the conversations between Terence and Donna that he'd overheard during that time. An unexpected perk of the job. He also smiled because in the process he'd struck a blow for exploited foreign workers. But more importantly, he'd ruined Terence's life.

Terence would wallow in his own misery for a while but Lemure couldn't bear to witness anything suffer for long, which is why he would soon put Terence out of his misery for good.

Chapter 13.

The outbreak happened quicker than Lemure had expected. The pies were delivered and on the shelves in hours after they left the factory so the first cases started to be reported only a couple of days later.

Three days after the pies left the factory, the newspapers, TV and radio were full of the story – one of the worst outbreaks of salmonella to hit Britain. There were fifty people in hospital, more being reported every day, although as yet, no-one had died. The medical experts were saying although it was salmonella, with all the unpleasant symptoms that entailed, it was a particularly mild strain. Everyone was expected to recover fully, even if they were a couple of clothing sizes smaller.

Not that that was giving much comfort to Terence as he paced about his office muttering: "We're buggered. We're buggered."

Donna had never seen Terence pace before. It wasn't a pretty sight. It was more like a sweaty walrus waddling about in a space that was too small for it.

'Still, look on the bright side," she thought, with a smile, 'My arse is safe, even if my job isn't.'

Terence had just taken another call from the environmental health inspector who'd visited the factory yesterday. He confirmed the outbreak was from Terence's factory and that it would be shut down for at least a couple of weeks while they established the exact source of the outbreak and cleaned up. They also had to recall all the pies that had left the factory since the original batch, in case they were infected too.

So far, his factory had not been mentioned in the media but the hyenas were closing in. They knew it was a food manufacturer in the North of England and within hours the name would be out. It was already common knowledge in the area that the inspectors had visited but that had not yet been reported.

Once his factory was sealed off and the recall notices were issued, he would no longer have a business. An outbreak like this in the food industry was the kiss of death, even for a healthy firm, but for a company as sick as Terence's there would be no re-opening after the factory was cleaned up. Even someone as stupid as Terence realised that. Then there was the court case. And even to Terence, it seemed inevitable they would also discover the phantom workers.

Terence shuddered. He felt cold even though he was sweating like a pig. He reached for his tablets and opened the bottle. It was empty. He knew he'd been eating them like sweets for the last week but he didn't realise he'd swallowed so many.

"Donna," he hollered. "Have you got any of my tablets through there?"

There was a pause while Donna looked in her desk drawer. She thought he'd used the last bottle on Monday but she checked just to be sure. He was bound to blow a fuse if there weren't any. He was in luck – there was a bottle in the drawer.

"Yes, there is a bottle here. I'll bring it through," she replied. "But go easy on those things they're stronger than you think."

"Since when did you become a bloody doctor and I don't need a lecture from you, woman," came the response.

'Ah well it's your funeral,' she thought prophetically, as she walked through to his office to give him the tablets.

Chapter 14.

Terence was sitting alone at the end of the bar. The barman was busy finding things to do at the other end. Terence on jovial form was hard enough to take, but Terence in a depressed state was purgatory.

The pub looked busier than it actually was, largely due to the five-yard exclusion zone which existed around Terence. Everyone else was grouped in the rest of the pub and no-one lingered at the bar after they'd been served. Some had avoided being sucked into Terence's vortex of despair by a tip-off from the barman, others had been pulled back from the brink when they quickly detected Terence's mood as they attempted to strike up a conversation.

Terence ordered another whiskey. He knew he'd had too many, especially considering his medication, but he had no idea how many. It really had been the worst day in Terence's life. His business had been closed down 'temporarily', but even Terence realised it would never re-open. The police were now involved and it seemed likely there would be charges resulting from the outbreak. And to top it off a terse phone conversation with Tony Rosling had ended his family's long-time involvement with the accountant. He simply could no longer weave any sort of magic over the accounts to keep Terence's head above water, and his own held high in society. Terence realised that without him, he was sunk. These were problems which would not go away naturally, so he was attempting to drink them away. It was proving harder than he thought.

Terence looked up from studying the amber liquid in his glass to see a swarthy looking man in a red Ferrari cap approach the bar. Terence looked at him for a moment and then even his will to strike up a conversation in the hope of some company deserted him too. His gaze returned to his glass and he began to contemplate whether he should order another before he finished this one, or wait until he finished it. His life's decisions were now very simple, but nevertheless still tricky for Terence.

"Good evening," said the guy in the baseball cap.

Terence looked up wearily and realised that the man was talking to him. Terence smiled. Two hours he'd been here and so far, everyone had done a runner as soon as Terence spoke to them. Now, here was someone who wanted to talk to him. Typical. Funny old world.

"Evening," replied Terence, almost too disillusioned now to want any company.

"You live here?" asked the man, who had a very strong Italian accent.

"More or less," replied Terence. "Usually on this stool to be exact."

"No, I mean in this region," clarified the Italian.

"This 'area' you mean," said Terence, who couldn't resist correcting people, largely because he so rarely got the opportunity to do so.

"Yes, fairly close. I run a ... I mean I have a business around here," said Terence, painfully aware that even his corrected version was not strictly accurate any more.

"Not the big pie factory?" said the Italian.

"Yes, that's the one," said Terence. "Over a couple of hundred employees," he added proudly, again quoting from the past before realising he'd have to change all his conversations now.

"Ah, that is lucky for me," said the Italian.

"Not so bloody lucky for me," muttered Terence.

"I was looking for the owner of that factory and someone said I might find him in here," continued the Italian who didn't seem to have heard Terence. "Now I find him immediately. That is lucky."

"Might be," said Terence. "Why are you looking for me?"

"I have a business deal for you," replied the Italian.

"A business deal? For me?" asked Terence.

The barman looked along the bar and saw the Italian talking to Terence. He considered tipping him the wink but he detected the man's accent and thought 'Sod it, he's foreign. He can do us all a favour and keep the Fat Man occupied. Keep the rest of the customers safe. Sort of an immigrant chore'. He smiled to himself. Still, the Italian was going to need a drink if he was going to cope with Terence and so the barman walked over to the pair.

"A deal to get you out of your present problems," said the Italian.

"How do you know I have problems?" asked Terence.

"Hah," the Italian laughed. "Everyone knows you have problems. But maybe only I can take care of them for you."

The Italian turned to the barman and said: "A beer and whatever my friend is drinking."

The barman nodded, reluctant to get involved in their conversation.

"And just how are you going to do that?" asked Terence.

"Maybe we should move to a table in that corner and I will explain my proposition."

"Fair enough," said Terrence. "You pick up the drinks and I'll have a pee before we talk business."

Terence slopped off his stool and waddled unsteadily to the toilets as the Italian paid for the drinks and carried them to the table.

When Terence returned, he seemed a little more composed. He'd obviously tried washing his hands and face in the hope of sobering up a little. The water had splashed down his shirt. But he did seem a little more alert as a result.

He took a sip of his whiskey and said: "So how can you fix my little problem then?"

The Italian explained: "Well I have some money, enough to end your money problems. I would like to own a factory in this area and yours seems like it could be for sale."

Terence was struggling to understand. Despite the Italian's strong accent his English was excellent. The problem was Terence was too shocked to take it all in. The amount he'd drunk wasn't helping his powers of comprehension either.

The Italian went on: "I know the factory is closed and I know it will be a while before it re-opens - if it does - but I just need an established business, even if it is in trouble, if you know what I mean."

Terence nodded although he wasn't sure he did know what the Italian meant. Maybe it was something to do with the mafia. Terence would have to be careful. His head was spinning. He did not know if it was from the whiskey or from the Italian's offer of a lifeline. He must be careful but then this could be the answer to all his problems – well to most of them anyway.

"I won't go into the details here in such a public place but perhaps we can talk tomorrow when you are a little more... er clear," said the Italian.

Terence just nodded. The spinning was getting worse. He needed to sleep this off and to get hold of Tony Rosling. If this was a decent deal Tony would be able to get the best out of it.

Terence shook his head, but that just made the spinning worse. The Italian was still talking and handing him a business card.

"We will talk tomorrow?" he asked.

"Yes, I'll ring you," said Terence, struggling to read the card. He slipped it into his pocket.

"Right now, I need to go home," slurred Terence.

"I can give you a lift if you want," offered Terence's prospective life saver.

"Aye, that would be good," replied Terence. "I think I've had one too many."

"It is always the last one that causes the problem," laughed the Italian, finishing his beer. "Not the one that came before, or the one before that. My car is just outside if you are ready to go."

"OK ta," said Terence as he got unsteadily to his feet, and began to weave his way across the pub.

The Italian was holding his arm, making them a very odd couple. A fat, drunk man and a bouncy Italian with a baseball cap and black leather jacket.

"I really enjoy English pubs," the Italian was saying, "Especially ones with real fires."

Terence bumped into a table. The couple at the table grabbed their glasses to stop them from spilling and glared at Terence. The Italian smiled at them and shrugged apologetically.

"Yes, I love a good fire," said Terence, as the pair lurched out of the pub.

Chapter 15.

Terence's head was thumping. He closed his eyes even tighter in the hope it would shut out the banging but it seemed to be getting louder. Terence put his head under the pillow but it was no use. Now there was a ringing sound too. Then he heard voices.

Through Terence's befuddled state he began to make sense of the cacophony of sounds that were splitting his head apart. Someone was banging on his door and ringing his doorbell, and whoever it was seemed to be shouting.

Terence slowly began to decipher the shouting.

"Mr Nicholson. It's the police. Open the door."

Terence stumbled out of bed, realising he was still fully dressed, and staggered to the door.

"OK stop banging, I'm coming," he shouted, and then immediately regretted it. He wished he'd just put up with the banging because it had hurt his head less than shouting back at them.

He opened the door to two uniformed officers.

"Can we come in please?" said the older of the two officers without any preamble or greeting.

"What do you want?" said Terence.

"We'd like to talk to you about an incident at your factory last night."

"An incident? What kind of incident?" asked Terence. "My factory is closed. There's nobody there to cause a bloody incident."

"If we could just come in, please, sir," persisted the older officer.

It was all too much for Terence to deal with in his present state. He'd hoped to be clearer in the morning after his binge last night, but he was worse. He turned around, walked into his living room and slumped into a chair. The pair followed and sat down.

"Were you anywhere near your factory last night sir?" asked the officer who'd done all the talking so far. The other officer took out his notepad.

"No, I was in the pub," replied Terence, as jigsaw pieces of the previous evening began to fall into some order.

"And after you left the pub?"

"I came back here and went to bed," he replied, although Terence couldn't actually find any of the jigsaw pieces that confirmed that.

"And were you alone sir?"

"Yes," began Terence, then he remembered the Italian. "Well, I was alone for most of the time in the pub," he said bitterly. "But I got a lift home from a … er, friend."

"And who would that be?" asked the officer.

Terence mumbled as his head swam.

'Shit', he thought, 'he had no idea who it was.' Then he remembered the business card. He slipped his podgy finger into his pocket and produced a card. Terence sighed and looked at the card. A wave of panic swept over him as he stared at the card. He dug his hands into both pockets but apart from a few coins they were empty.

"Sir?" said the policeman.

Terence did not know what to say and the card from the local takeaway that he was looking at was no help to him in identifying his mystery friend.

"Er I can't remember his name," mumbled Terence. "I only met him last night."

"I see sir, and this is the gentleman who gave you a lift home is it?"

"That's right," said Terence, painfully aware how weak that sounded.

"And have you any idea what time you got home?"

"No, not really, about 1030, elevenish, I think. I'd had a few, you see," said Terence, hoping that would explain everything. But instead of simply smiling and exchanging 'jack-the-lad' grins before leaving, the pair sat stony-faced and asked another question.

"Do you recall the kind of car your 'friend' was driving, sir?"

"Look what is all this about?" exploded Terence, hoping that would restore some of his diminishing credibility. But his head pounded and he lost the will to keep his anger at boiling point.

"The car, sir," continued the policeman. "What kind was it?"

"It was a red one," answered Terence, "Some sort of sports car."

Terence recalled how difficult it had been for him to fit his bulky frame into such a small car.

"Registration number?" asked the policeman.

Terence shook his head. It was all too much of a blur.

"And did your .... er friend, stay the night?" asked the policeman with what seemed to Terence like the beginning of a smug grin on his face.

"What the hell are you suggesting?" Terence exploded, his head exploding immediately afterwards.

"I'm not suggesting anything, sir, just trying to jog your memory about your friend in the hope we can help you identify him," the policeman replied, the smirk still in place.

"Look what is this all about?" Terence asked again.

"It's about a fire sir," said the officer. "A fire at your factory."

"A fire?" said Terence. "What bloody fire? Nobody has contacted me about a fire."

"We tried to contact you sir, but there was no reply, so we contacted the other key holder, a Mr...." The policeman looked in his pocketbook.

"A Mr Rosling," he added. "He attended the scene, although he told us he was no longer officially associated with the business."

"But, but.." Terence stammered, trying to make sense of his crumbling life. "What about my factory?"

"Oh, it was a relatively small fire, sir," answered the policeman. "A local resident noticed it very quickly and raised the alarm. Just some damage to a couple of smaller buildings, not the main factory, although it could have spread there very quickly if it had not been brought under control so sharply."

Terence sighed and slumped back into his chair.

"However, there are some other matters we would like to investigate," said the policemen.

"Like how it started?" asked Terence.

"Not really," the officer replied. "We are fairly sure we know how it started. We are more interested in 'why' it started."

"I don't understand," stuttered Terence.

"Really sir?" said the policemen. "We rather hoped you would understand and that you'd be able to help us to understand."

"Me? I wasn't there," said Terence. "I didn't even know there was a fire until you woke me up and told me."

"So you say sir," replied the officer.

"Then how can I help," continued Terence.

"Well, you could start by telling us who your friend in the red sports car is," said the first policemen.

"What's that got to do with it?" snapped Terence. "I told you before he gave me a lift and then went home." Although as Terence was saying this, he had a sudden flashback of the man standing in his bedroom. He had an image of him standing there as Terence lay, collapsed on the bed. Terence shut the image out of his mind. That was a rabbit hole he had no wish to go down at the moment when so much other nonsense was going on around him.

"Home sir?" said the policeman. "And where would that be then?"

"I don't bloody know. Can we forget about him for now. I thought you were here to talk about my fire."

"Oh, we are talking about 'your' fire, sir" said the first policemen. "Perhaps it would make matters clearer for you if I told you the resident who raised the alarm was so quick in noticing the fire that they actually saw the person who started it."

"Someone started it?" said Terence incredulously. It had never occurred to his pedestrian brain that the fire had been started by someone, and not something, like an electrical fault or something overheating.

"That's right sir," added the policeman. "A man in a red sports car."

What was left of Terence's world shattered. He could actually hear a sound like a plate glass window shattering.

"Do you have the keys to your factory sir?" he heard the policeman ask through the noise of the breaking glass.

Terence was too numb to speak. His confusion had reached new depths. He struggled to put the pieces in place and make sense of it all.

The man in the sports car had torched his factory. But he had wanted to buy it. Why would he try to destroy something that he wanted to own? Perhaps he was trying to reduce the price. No, that was crazy. The price could not get much lower given the state of his business.

Terence stumbled across the room to the drawer where he kept the factory keys. They weren't there. He rummaged in the drawer, but still, he could not find them. He checked his pockets, forgetting that they were empty when he'd checked them earlier for the mystery Italian's business card. They were still empty.

"Er, perhaps they're in the bedroom," said Terence, panicking. He turned to go and check. He froze. Before him stood the first policeman.

"Are these what you're looking for sir?" he asked.

In his hand were Terence's factory keys. He recognised the keyring with the words 'The Boss' clearly visible. Terence nodded.

"Where did you get those?" asked Terence.

"I think you'd better come with us sir..", was the only explanation.

Terence again heard the sound of shattering glass in his head and then a thumping like he'd never heard before, as he was only vaguely aware of the policeman reading him his rights as he was arrested.

Chapter 16.

Lemure turned off the TV. He had just watched a well put-together report on the local news. It was a comprehensive roundup of the collapse of Terence's business. The reporter had done a very thorough job of pulling together the various disparate strands and had woven them into a compelling piece of TV. The financial difficulties, the salmonella outbreak, the unhealthy lifestyle and an illuminating interview with a couple who remembered Terence mentioning his fondness for fires as he'd left the pub with the police's only arson suspect the night before the fire.

Lemure was impressed that so much of the story had become apparent in only a few days. It was very comprehensive and managed to stay on the right side of the laws of contempt and libel. Actually, neither were a major risk anymore, as the police still had not arrested the man suspected of starting this fire, and Terence was no longer under arrest. His sudden death as a result of a heart attack had ended that particular line of judicial inquiry and removed the threat of libel with Terence's mortality.

Lemure walked over to his computer and turned it on.

'It was amazing how things could snowball once they were off and running,' he thought as he watched the screen come to life. Lemure had been content to simply ruin Terence's life, ending it completely was an unexpected bonus. He typed in his password. Of course, Terence's heart condition and obesity were a major factor and the substituted medication may also have played a part.

Soon Lemure would have to pack up and go home, making sure to remove all trace that he'd ever been there but first he looked at the screen of his laptop. He smiled as he looked at a list of names. The top one was already crossed out. Lemure now proceeded to cross out the second one – Terence Nicholson - and he closed the laptop.

Chapter 17.

The bell went and everyone began to gather up their books and belongings.

"I never told anyone to move," bawled the intimidating voice of James Collins, history teacher and pain in the arse.

"I'll tell you when my lesson ends," he shouted.

'Pompous prick', thought Porky. He knows the other teachers will be just as insistent that everyone arrives on time for their lesson as he is about punctuality for his lessons. So how could they be expected to arrive on time, if he prevented them from leaving his lessons on time.

Although, this time Collins's pomposity could go on as long as he wanted it to, as far as Porky was concerned. He hated Collins's lessons, even though he loved history. But he dreaded the next lesson even more than staying behind with old Collins.

"Right, slowly gather up your belongings," Collins was saying, somewhat redundantly as everyone had already done that the moment they heard the bell.

"Now without running, form an orderly line and proceed to your next lesson – quietly," he added.

Porky sighed, his temporary reprieve was over.

"And make sure you're not late," added Collins, seemingly oblivious to the irony of his warning.

The noise level increased instantly the group of excited boys were outside the history room because, unlike Porky, the next lesson was a highlight of their week, and, almost as one, the group began to run down the hill towards the swimming pool.

They were heading for 40 minutes of swimming – the lesson that everyone looked forward to all week, almost as much as Porky dreaded it. He was one of three boys in the class who couldn't swim.

One of the other two was such a pathetic wimp that it was taken as read that he wouldn't be able to swim. He couldn't do anything and often arrived with a sick note that excused him from even attempting whatever sport was lined up for them for that day. Porky had no such excuse. He could not simply get his mother to write a letter or even forge one as the other boys did if they needed to be away early on a Friday, or miss games to nip into town. Porky had to convince Matron that he was sick. There were people in hospices who would fail to clear that hurdle, finding themselves on their way out of her surgery doubting their own symptoms after a dose of penicillin, or a couple of aspirins.

The other non-swimmer was a strange boy. A loner, who should be the butt of a thousand jokes but rarely was; a boy who was reasonably good at other sports but not swimming; an unremarkable scholar - in fact, average in most things, apart from being odd.

Porky began to get undressed. He looked around the changing room. Nearly everyone was already changed so he began tearing off his clothes, not because of a surge of enthusiasm but because he did not want to incur the wrath of Smoothie Slater by being last into the pool.

Actually, only Smoothie thought he was smooth. In fact, he was an archetypal, sadistic PE teacher – tall, athletic, lived in a tracksuit, hair never out of place and taught geography. Was geography so easy that even Neanderthals could teach it? All PE teachers seemed to have that as their academic speciality. It never seemed to be that easy for Porky when it came to geography exam time.

Smoothie Slater was bad enough posing about on a rugby pitch, but equipped with a whistle in a swimming pool, he was pure evil.

"Come on you lot, hurry up and line up on the edge of the pool," he said, stalking into the changing room.

Everyone filed into the pool, with the inevitable pushing and shoving as they walked along the edge, in the hope that someone would fall in.

Porky never understood this. Of course, he could see it was funny if someone fell in the water but he also knew that Smoothie could not fail to see and hear the splash. His first words would be "Get out, you moron," followed quickly by "Who pushed him?" If there was no response and the premature swimmer was not forthcoming with a name, then he would make everyone sit on the side of the pool until the power of peer pressure forced a name into the open.

Porky loved it when no-one owned up. He'd even wished he had the guts to throw himself into the water and then sit out the whole lesson because no-one could own up. But his fear of the water prevented such subterfuge.

Once, Smoothie had made them all go back into the changing room and get dressed, not allowing them to swim at all that lesson. That had been Porky's favourite lesson, although he'd trudged back into the changing room, muttering oaths against Smoothie under his breath like everyone else.

Porky sighed. Everyone had made it safely along the side of the pool and they were all sitting down on the edge of the pool, waiting for the command to get in. Porky had seen people fall in even at *this late stage, but it was rare. He knew what was coming next. The ritual humiliation.*

"OK so who is it in this class who can't swim," Smoothie asked, looking towards the shallow end where Porky and the other two land-lovers were cowering.

Three hands went into the air and at least a dozen sniggers rippled along the line of amphibians.

"Right, well apart from you three," said Smoothie. "I want the rest of you in the pool." A huge splash interrupted his sentence.

"Wait for it, you moron, get out and sit on the side, Stevenson. Did anyone push him?" asked Smoothie.

Silence.   Porky groaned. Tottingham was grinning like a Cheshire cat. Of course, someone pushed him. Why couldn't they all sit out while the culprit was identified?   However, Smoothie obviously thought Stevenson had just leapt on the ambiguity of his words to take a flyer, so gave up on trying to find the culprit.

"As I was saying," he continued. "When I blow my whistle, I want ten widths, going in pairs.

"Nicholson, you wallow your way across five times as you don't have a partner." The sniggers flowed up the line again.

Smoothie blew his whistle and it was like the start of the cup final. The noise level exploded. Half the class splashed into the pool, and the other half took that as a cue to start shouting.

Smoothie walked down the length of the pool towards the non-swimmers.

"Right get in the water, you lot," he said. "And let's see how far you can get." This was the extent of the swimming tuition.

"OK Pye, you first," said Smoothie.

Porky slid into the pool and set off for the other side. He was determined to get across this time.

He took three feeble strokes and then began to sink. His foot dropped to the floor of the pool and he hopped another yard. Porky hoped no-one had seen the hop-assisted stroke.

"Get your bloody feet up, Pye," bellowed Smoothie.

Porky kicked again but he was only half way across when he sank. He surfaced spluttering to hear Smoothie say: "That was even more pathetic than usual. You can do that again after Marsden and Simpson."

Porky coughed and trudged his way to the side of the pool, sneaking a look at the clock as he went.

Marsden was a weedy little specimen who could normally be relied on to be even more pathetic than Porky. Off he went. Porky leaned against the side of the pool. Marsden looked like a daddy-longlegs trying to get out of the water. His arms and legs were going in all directions and his head was thrashing about from side to side, but amazingly he was moving slowly towards the other side of the pool.

Porky was torn. Part of him really willed Marsden to do it, but part of him realised that if he did, then Porky would become even more conspicuous and pathetic as a result.

Marsden was three-quarters of the way across when he too sank under the surface. He emerged a couple of seconds later, coughing and spluttering. Porky breathed a sigh of relief but immediately joined Simpson in saying well done to the drowned insect as he made his way back to the edge.

Simpson made it almost as far as Marsden, which is as far as he usually got. He'd made no discernible progress since he arrived at the school but seem unperturbed by his stalemate. Porky often wondered if Simpson did it on purpose. He was such a weird child that Porky would not be surprised to discover he could

73

swim all along, and deliberately only made it three-quarters of the way across just to be awkward.

"Finished sir." "Me too" began the voices at the deep end of the pool.

This was what Porky had feared, the other boys were finishing their swim and would probably be told to sit on the side of the pool while the three class members without gills were forced to try again.

"Well sit on the edge until everyone has finished," said Smoothie, predictably. "Right Pye, off you go again."

Porky was painfully aware of more and more pairs of restless eyes with nothing better to do than watch him drown. He kicked off and began to thrash his arms and legs wildly. He could sense it wasn't going to work before he started swallowing water. Still, he kicked and splashed with his arms, only vaguely aware of a voice shouting: "Go on, kick!"

Porky kicked but he went nowhere. Well, that wasn't strictly true, he went down. Eventually, he had to drop his feet and come up for air. His head roared with the sound of laughter, and then just as he was catching his breath a wave of water hit him in the face as something landed in the water in front of him. The laughter went off the audio scale.

"Who threw that?" yelled Smoothie, although as Porky wiped the water from his face he was sure he saw a smirk at the corner of Slater's mouth.

"Come on, who was it?" he repeated.

A hand went up towards the deep end of the pool.

"I thought he was drowning sir so I threw it to rescue him," said Stevenson, grinning, even though he was trying to fake

sincerity in his voice. The full-sized industrial lifebelt was still bobbing in front of Porky.

"I'll decide if he's drowning, you moron," said Smoothie. "You could have taken his head off throwing that from there."

The laughter, which had subsided a little, flared back up again.

"Right give it here, Pye, and then keep practising while the others have another swim," said Smoothie, holding out his arm for the lifebelt.

Practising. Porky didn't mind practising because it usually meant being ignored for the rest of the lesson, although he knew it would never help teach him to swim.

Marsden and his daddy long legs plopped into the water and thrashed about, while Simpson smiled and set off splashing towards the other side of the pool.

Chapter 18.

Lemure sighed contentedly as he walked into his apartment. It was modern, luxurious but sparse. Everything in there was high quality, but functional. There were no photographs or ornaments. Everything earned its right to be in Lemure's life, or it was removed.

He switched on the lights and settled down in front of his computer. He allowed himself the luxury of letting his mind wander as the machine booted up. The screen opened on the page he'd been viewing before he left his temporary 'Nicho home' - his base while he'd carried out his recent pursuit of Terence Nicholson.

Lemure's eyes again landed on the name at the top of the list - already crossed out on his screen – David Stevenson or 'Stevo'' as he was known at school, and throughout the early part of his adult life. The third part of the triumvirate which had made school life for so many boys far from the best days of their lives. Admittedly, he was by far the weakest link, and Lemure had to accept that in different circumstances, he might have been very different - a friend even?

'No, he would never have been a friend,' Lemure concluded. But he would almost certainly not have been an enemy – a malignant force which lingered and festered in the memory of so many, long after they had left school and gone their separate ways. Ironic then that he'd been the first to die and the one to give Lemure a new purpose in life.

Lemure remembered making one of his infrequent trips back to the town where his school played such a central role in his life. He was sitting in one of the pubs they used to frequent as sixth-formers, and occasionally as fifth-formers. They only ever used pubs which were carefully selected. They were always in side streets, always had at least two exits and were usually frequented by old men, rather than places where younger teachers may go. They were havens; places to while away the evenings drinking cheap bitter, playing darts or pool, and talking to friends. They were home to some of Lemure's happiest memories of his time at school. That was why he liked to return occasionally, although he never saw any of today's schoolboys frequenting the same sort of places.

'Probably moved up-market', he thought. 'Trendy wine bars and the like. Possibly the teachers were less concerned about underage drinking and so today's pupils could be less furtive and more sociable'.

He had unfolded the local newspaper and looked at the front page. Lemure had audibly gasped. He was used to seeing articles about former school friends, and foes alike, especially in reports of local rugby and cricket teams, which often included many of the day-boys who still lived locally. But this was a shocker.

Right across the front page was the headline 'STEGS Boy in Freak Diving Tragedy' and underneath was a photograph of a man in diving gear smiling at the camera and putting his thumb up in the time-honoured pose so beloved of local newspaper photographers. The photograph appeared to have been taken nearby, perhaps on the coast near the school, suggesting that the diver was serious about his sport because diving in the Irish Sea was not a feat to be taken lightly. But it was the man's face which had made Lemure gasp. He quickly scanned the text of the article for confirmation of his suspicion.

There it was. In the second paragraph. 'David Stevenson, 32, a former pupil of St Elizabeth's Grammar School, was a diving instructor on the Thai island of Koh Samui.'

Lemure quickly read the whole article, which continued on to page three. He then re-read it slowly. Putting the paper down, he took a long drink of his pint.

David Stevenson was dead. The circumstances were bizarre. It seems the one-time tormentor and would-be life-guard had become a diving instructor on Koh Samui, where he'd worked for three years. He'd taught hundreds of divers and accompanied hundreds more on trips to exotic-sounding places, like Shark Island and Sail Rock. Lemure was familiar with the area and had even dived there himself, after eventually learning to swim in the final years at school.

It appears David Stevenson had been on one of these day trips when tragedy struck. He'd been diving with a group of experienced divers, near Koh Tao, an island about one and a half hours speedboat ride north of Koh Samui.

They were diving at about 30 metres, way below the levels of normal holiday divers. Stevo had gone down first and settled on the bottom to wait for the others to equalise the pressure in their ears and get down to him. He'd sunk to his knees on the sandy seabed and landed on a pair of venomous stonefish. Their spines pierced his wetsuit and injected their deadly poison into his legs. He'd lost consciousness before any of the other divers had reached him. In fact, it was thought he could have been unconscious for more than a minute before anyone had realised there was a problem.

The other divers had immediately taken him back to the surface, although they had to do it slowly to avoid adding decompression sickness to David's problems. Ironically, Koh Samui is one of the few Thai islands equipped with a hyperbaric chamber for treating decompression sickness and other diving related conditions. That had been one of the reasons Stevo had chosen it as his diving base.

Unfortunately, this was of little comfort in this case, as what David needed was a shot of vaccine against the poison. He got one, but only when the rescue boat from Koh Samui had made the hour-long trip to Koh Tao, a delay which proved fatal.

A doctor specialising in diving conditions was quoted as saying this would not necessarily have been a problem with a single sting, but David had received a massive dose of venom in both legs, and so the vaccine had failed to revive him. He died on the rescue boat on his way back to Koh Samui.

Lemure was genuinely shocked. Not by the death of a classmate; nor by the bizarre circumstances of his death; but by the warm glow he'd experienced as he read of Stevo's death. He really did not think he'd hated him that much but he was actually relieved he was dead, almost happy.

Lemure's mind flashed back to those swimming baths, almost twenty years earlier, when the fish-like Stevenson had thrown a lifebelt and mocked the pathetic attempts of the non swimmers.

Stevenson, born to military parents and brought up in numerous hot climates had learned to swim almost before he could walk and so it was beyond his comprehension how anyone could have got to thirteen and still not been able to swim. To him, it was like still crawling on your hands and knees, rather than walking.

'Ironic', Lemure thought, 'that his life should be ended by a fellow water dweller'.

But Lemure's mind was now racing and he felt his life change forever as he sat in that dingy pub in a northern town. He began to relive all the unhappy moments of his school days. They flooded before his eyes like a drowning man. He felt anger like he'd never felt before.

The warm glow he'd felt at discovering Stevo was dead was being replaced by a burning rage at how unhappy he'd been for eight years, thanks to the damage inflicted by a small group. It was amazing to him how so few could make so many, so miserable, for so long, so easily.

Well, now the stonefish had struck back on behalf of them all. Perhaps Lemure should assume the responsibility that was rightfully his and continue the work begun by those stonefish.

Lemure took another long drink of his pint, and felt it cool his mouth and throat, as it began to quench the raging heat in the rest of his body. It was like a drug flowing through his veins, calming him and replacing his anger with cool determination.

Lemure felt a power he'd never felt before. He had a clear purpose. He had a mission and it was a just one. He closed his eyes and smiled. At that moment, Lemure was conceived. His actual birth would, of course, be about nine months later, but that was the moment Lemure's life had really begun.

Lemure turned off his computer and stretched. He looked at his watch. It was 8 pm. He was hungry.

'To eat in, or to have some fun?' that was the question he was toying with.

He looked in the fridge. It contained only the basics because he had not yet shopped since his return home. Decision made. But what did he fancy tonight?

Lemure's choices of food were often far more far-reaching than simply opting for Chinese, or Indian. There was all the associated paraphernalia to be considered.

Eating out was also Lemure's time for role play; his time to hone his skills; to perfect the art of deception and then, to disappear into the shadows, yet again. He usually adopted a character, sometimes complete with disguise, and the experience could last for days. But he decided he was not really in the mood for a long exercise at the moment. A one-off training run would be enough for tonight. Besides he was anxious to get started on his next project.

'Tonight's meal would simply be an exercise in disguise, carried out at a local Italian restaurant, where they recognised him by sight, if not by name', he concluded. 'But who should he be?'

He felt like adopting the appearance of an old man - perhaps a Polish refugee - who would cantankerously act out the evening without anyone suspecting the difficult old man was in fact, the smart, polite young man who often called in, but always ate alone.

Lemure smiled as he walked to his dressing room. He loved dressing up, and this character would involve make-up, wig, speech and an appropriate walk – pretty much the full range.

He liked playing old men. They posed a satisfying challenge. The only problem was that, although he could flirt like mad without women taking offence, he could never capitalise on the openings his performance created for him. On numerous occasions, he had passed up the opportunity of a night with a stunning woman because he was obliged to stay in character.

Sometimes Lemure suffered for his art. But then it was more than an art - he had a purpose, a cause - something he had devoted himself to. And that was way more important than casual sex.

Chapter 19.

Lemure returned home after a remarkably uneventful evening. Of course, he had passed off his disguise without being recognised, but that went without saying now that he had become so proficient.

It had not always been so, with a couple of disastrous early adventures that went horribly wrong, but now it was always flawless. There had been no drama, no excitement, no need to think on his feet - nada! So what was the point? Practise, perfectionism and a commitment to his long-term goals.

Lemure was very aware of the risk of complacency and of his compulsion for risk-taking. He constantly had to fight his temptation to crank up the risk levels just to make things more interesting. It was difficult for him to accept it just wasn't worth it. His bigger plan was simply that: bigger and more important. He could not risk that by messing up during a practice session.

Still, it had been a pleasant evening and he'd enjoyed confusing the pretty young waitress who'd had the misfortune to serve the old Polish man. He'd completely ruined her evening and had no chance to make her night as he was in character. Shame, but that was the cost of perfection. She was a little scrawny for his taste anyway, so perhaps it was no big loss.

He let himself into his flat and as he did, his walk changed back to his normal gait and his demeanour returned to his own. He was himself again - whatever that meant.

In effect, Lemure had not been himself for years and he wasn't sure if he ever would be again. His life had become a lie - an irony not lost on him. He had pledged himself to fight lies, betrayal and deceit after he saw first hand the devastating effects they had on people - including himself. And yet, here he was using all three without a care for those caught up in his web of subterfuge.

Lemure poured himself a drink - gin and tonic, ice with a slice of lime, not lemon. It was hardly a martini, shaken not stirred, but then James Bond was so pretentious and out of touch with the real world of deception, it seemed more appropriate for Lemure to adopt a more popular, although not 'common', drink. Lemure could never accept 'common'.

He turned on some music - Pink Floyd instrumental - good to think to, nothing which would distract his thoughts.

Lemure considered it was time to take stock, consider what had been achieved and what still had to be done. It was important things were done in a logical manner, carefully planned and perfectly executed.

His mind flashed back to when he read that article about David Stevenson's death. At that point, it had only sparked the idea of exacting revenge on the other schoolyard tormentors. And at that point, he had no reason to extend his activities to others. No-one else had deserved it by then. So his thoughts had remained on school and school-related activities. Which was how the name James Collins had come back into his mind.

Collins had been a history teacher, a nasty vindictive little man with a complete absence of humour and a belief that his main purpose on this earth was to make sure everyone respected him. Well, no doubt he regarded it as respect - fear would be a more accurate description.

School folklore had it that when Collins first qualified as a teacher he'd been very different - reasonable, friendly and approachable. But he'd been the victim of the pack. Older boys had made his life hell - bullied him - until he'd suffered some form of breakdown.   On his return to the classroom, he'd become the monster that he was in later years.

Lemure didn't buy it.   Everything about Collins - his clothes, mannerisms, demeanour and his attitude - all pointed towards 'prick with a chip on his shoulder'.   Lemure imagined he was probably like it as a baby. Granted he had not spent very long checking the story, but it didn't seem to stack up.

Firstly, no-one could actually remember the incident, they all only knew someone who knew someone who said it had happened. But the most convincing evidence was when Lemure accessed Collins's medical records and there was no reference to any breakdown or even to any incident which could be interpreted as a breakdown.   That was good enough for Lemure.   And it was good enough to get James Collins added to Lemure's hit list.

And that is how it had remained for months - Nicholson, Tottingham and Collins.   But that was before his wife, Diana, had destroyed his world.   Her act of betrayal had caused him to re-think his list.   Her deceit was why the name of Rupert Burns was now also alongside Nicholson, Tottingham and Collins.

Burns was the odious little toad who was complicit in his wife's infidelity and the one she'd gone running to the moment Lemure found out and kicked her out without a penny.   Well, it was going to cost him much more than the price of pandering to her whims before Lemure was finished with him.   He had considered adding Diana to the list too but had rejected it as being too obvious a link to him.   Although perhaps a part of him could not forget that he'd once loved her. Perhaps he would change his mind and add her at a later date. You could say she was first reserve for now.

The decision he now had to make was determining the order in which he should progress through the list.

Who should be next? He'd already decided Tottingham would be the grand finale so that made it a decision between the two new additions to his list - Collins or Burns.

No doubt Burns would give Lemure greater satisfaction as he'd not only get revenge on a person who'd wronged him, but the effects of that revenge would affect Diana too.

But then, Burns was a traffic warden, as befits people of his ilk. The slightest problem and he'd squeal to the police or to anyone who would listen, and who might be able to defend him.

That didn't bother Lemure too much. He didn't have a particularly high regard for the police, but one or two of them were bright and there was no point alerting them to something of which they were currently totally ignorant.

Collins would also be easier, was more topical and some of the work had already been done, so Lemure had all he needed to wreak havoc on Collins's life, whereas he needed a little more preparation for Burns.

So, it looked like Lemure had made his decision. Burns was going nowhere and could wait. His wrongdoing was more recent and was still raw and painful to Lemure.

Collins's wrongdoing went back decades and his victims were far more numerous. He was getting older and it would be a missed opportunity if Lemure's inaction allowed him to die unpunished. He was also more in keeping with Lemure's original goals.

Lemure smiled, finished his drink and went to bed. Tomorrow was going to be a fun day.

Chapter 20.

Lemure woke at 7 am and went for a run, before showering and eating breakfast while catching up on the day's news.

As usual, there was an extended package on refugees from Syria, Iraq and other war-torn countries and the effect they were supposedly having on their host countries.

Lemure smiled. Not because he did not have sympathy for the refugees. He did. He had enormous sympathy and support for them and could not understand the animosity they were receiving from people who had never been anywhere more dangerous than a handbags bar brawl. The other day he'd heard a politician opposed to allowing more refugees into the country say: 'I mean, they've all got mobile phones' as if that somehow proved they were affluent travellers who simply chose to switch countries.

'Of course, some of them had mobile phones,' thought Lemure. 'They're from the Middle East, not the Middle Ages. If you were deciding which small items of value you were going to take with you when you fled your country, I suspect your mobile would be the choice of most people.

'No, Lemure smiled because the Not In My Backyard anti-refugee sentiment that was being fuelled by certain politicians in the run-up to the next election played right into his hands for how he was going to deal with James Collins.

James Collins had also earned the right to be next in Lemure's crosshairs partly because it suited his mood but also it did not require any travel.

This stage of his plan could be executed from the comfort of his home, thanks to the powers of the internet. The downside was he wouldn't get a chance to dress up and look his victim in the eye. But he really needed to spend some time at home, be seen locally and gather the cloak of respectability around himself again.

In addition, if Lemure was honest with himself he did not really want to look into Collins's eyes. He was now an old man and Lemure did not trust his resolve if he found time had not been kind to his former history teacher.

'No, better to do this one from a distance,' thought Lemure as he opened the folder named Anti Christ, which he'd now moved to his desktop.

Of course like all Lemure's computer equipment and programs, it was heavily encrypted but it now revealed a number of articles, an email history and a Twitter and Facebook account in the name of James Collins with regular postings over the past few months. There was some family stuff, photos and the like, which Lemure had got from a thorough search of the old man's computer, and some snippets about trips he'd made which Lemure had mainly got from his email account. There was also a series of more historic, academic articles. Most of them linked to blog posts on academic websites. The articles followed a pattern which had been increasing in frequency over the past few weeks, and were logically argued and well written.

Lemure skimmed the comment section a couple of the postings and saw the temperature was hotting up. A couple of academics had started to disagree and get a little more hot-under-the-collar with Collins's views.

'A storm in a port glass for academics,' Lemure mused and began to read the articles.

The first was very well balanced and tackled the issue of Islam and whether it, or any other religion, could truly claim to be non-violent. It was fair, well reasoned and referenced the oft-quoted comment that most wars had religion as an element.

Lemure noted that Collins had held back from claiming 'all' wars and from claiming religion was the cause - both allegations that were often made.

The next article expounded on this theme and introduced the influence various doctrines had on terrorist groups, like ISIS and Al-Qaeda.

The next went a little further and quoted the Qu'ran. It claimed the Day of Judgement would be preceded by the appearance of the Mahdi, or 'guided one', who would rid the world of evil.

Lemure reflected that Collins had bent reality a little here because he was not aware of any direct reference to the Mahdi in the Qu'ran. He speculated that most of Collins's audience would not know this, and if they did, they would probably extend him the academic leeway that there were many references to the Mahdi in numerous Islamic writings, if not the Qu'ran.

The article went on to 'explain' that the Mahdi's reign would coincide with the Second Coming of Jesus Christ (Isa) and together they would defeat the false messiah, or antichrist, (Masih ad-Dajjal).

Lemure began to read the next article which suggested this run up to the Day of Judgement had already started, citing the conflict in Syria as evidence, and quoting Islamic literature which stated that this would be the scene of the battle which preceded the final conflict.

Collins pointed out that the terrorist group ISIS had attached great importance to the Syrian town of Dabiq, a seemingly insignificant town near Aleppo.   ISIS had even named its propaganda magazine after the town.

He claimed that Islamic prophecy proclaimed that it would be in Dabiq where the armies of Islam would meet the armies of Rome - or Western allies as Collins claimed - and it was there that Islam would defeat the enemies of their faith.   That defeat would spark the countdown to the apocalypse, but not before the Islamic armies invaded and took Constantinople - now Istanbul.

After that victory, Collins claimed Islamic writings predicted the Islamic invasion would suffer a set-back. This would come in the form of the arrival of the Anti-Christ (Dajjal) from eastern Iran. He would almost wipe out the Islamic armies leaving only 5000 fighters holed up in Jerusalem.

At this point, cue the Second Coming. Jesus (Isa) would return to earth, kill Dajjal and lead the Muslims to victory.

Collins argued that in order for this prophesied outcome to come about, a couple of things were necessary, and they were already in place.

Firstly, he argued that Muslims had to be under attack from non-Muslims - check, that was now very apparent.

Secondly, they had to be defending a homeland, or more particularly, a caliphate - an Islamic state ruled by a caliph - check, that had been established by ISIS in Syria and Iraq.

So, Collins argued that as long as there was a caliphate Muslims would be obliged to defend it, indeed they had a duty to do so. This enabled recruiters to create Islamic armies which would prepare for the arrival of the crusading Western armies, and so trigger the end-game which, although brutal, would result in an overwhelming victory for Islam.

If Collins had left his articles at this point, they would be little more than boring religious articles by a former teacher, destined to be ignored.

He, or others, could have used Collins's research and theory as a platform to discuss the advisability of sending in ground troops which could be argued would only give the terrorists the non-Muslim army they were waiting to defeat.

He could have used it to speculate on the best way of destroying the caliphate, arguing that if the caliphate did not exist then there would be no Islamic state to defend. This would severely damage ISIS propaganda and affect its power to recruit because without a caliphate to defend there would be no need for an army to defend it, and so the end-game in Jerusalem could not play out as predicted.

Either option could be argued as constructive and something which should be debated, not only in the rarefied atmosphere of the halls of academia, but also in the corridors of power - if it was ever drawn to their attention.

Indeed, if the articles had been written by James Collins that is probably what would have happened. But these articles were written by Lemure and so they were certainly not going to stop here. They were now going to go in a very different, far more incendiary direction, and if Lemure's predictions were correct, trigger an apocalyptic end-game for James Collins.

Chapter 21.

Ricky Marriott picked up his pint and walked to a table in a quiet corner of the pub. Not that any part of the pub was busy at that time of day - after the lunchtime crowd and before the after-work rush.

He took a long drink, savoured the taste, swallowed and opened his laptop. The fact his machine automatically connected to the pub's WIFI network gave away the truth that this was Ricky's unofficial office. It was his quiet spot, his meeting place, his get-away-from the mayhem sanctuary. It was a place where he could actually take some time away from constant deadlines to think.

The internet - and mobile phones - had changed his working life beyond recognition. He used to visit pubs to find a phone, now he could be reached wherever he was, and visiting the pub was frowned upon.

He used to have deadlines to work towards but now the online version of his newspaper meant there was always a deadline looming.

The Brown Cow may have a good WIFI signal, but its mobile network was very poor, providing a convenient 'out of circulation' status when needed. And above all, it provided Ricky with a chance to partake of his favourite hobby - real ale.

Ricky took another more thoughtful sip of his pint as he began to read the article on his laptop.

It was an online report from a local newspaper 100 miles across the Pennines in Yorkshire, something he would not have been able to find, or read as easily without the internet, Ricky had to grudgingly accept.

Ricky read with interest because the story was about someone he knew, someone he had gone to school with. It was the latest report on the downfall of Terence Nicholson, charting his financial difficulties, the poisoning outbreak and investigations into the factory fire.

Ricky read it with interest, punctuated only by the occasional sip of his pint.

Ricky had found out about Terence's death a few days earlier and had written a short piece about it for his paper along the lines of former local schoolboy dies somewhere else. It was one of those dubious articles, done on the premise that he'd be known by some school friends who still lived in the area.

But Terence had never lived in the area, and to Ricky's knowledge Terence had never even been back to the town since he left school almost 20 years ago and so he didn't really have many friends there.

Still, it was an article of record, rather than of interest, and his editor felt it was too weak a link to justify the inclusion of the interesting stuff about the fires and poisoning. Ricky's article had mentioned those facts in passing but it was little more than a factual obituary recording the death of a man who once attended the town's main school.

Ricky's fascination with Terence's circumstances had started as mainly personal, but it was starting to become more professional. Ricky had been the journalist who had written the story about the death of David Stevenson, who'd been killed in a bizarre diving accident in Thailand. David and Terence had been in the same year at St Elizabeth's. They'd been in the same boarding house.

They'd been part of the same friendship group, or was gang a better word, for the duration of their stay at school.

Ricky knew this because he'd been there for the whole seven years. He wasn't part of their gang. He'd been a couple of years younger. He'd never been a particular target of their bullying, for which he was very grateful, but he knew how others had suffered. He'd seen it first hand, experienced it a couple of times, and he'd watched as victims had withered under the onslaught, watched as some of them cried themselves to sleep.

Ricky took another long drink of his pint, swallowed and sighed. He scratched his head and turned over the details in his mind.

Two members of the same gang dead. Both died in bizarre circumstances. But died in different parts of the world and the deaths were unrelated.

Ricky had no idea why he felt the way he did. Part of him had little sympathy for the pair. They had been difficult to like at school. Ricky assumed they'd continued to behave the same way after they left school and so had probably remained difficult to like.

And yet he felt uneasy about the story. But 'uneasy' was nowhere close to justifying an article. This was why Ricky had decided to review everything once again in the sanctuary of The Brown Cow. One final review before he concluded there was no story.

Ricky looked at his watch, finished the dregs of his pint and shut his laptop. All the evidence pointed towards an unhappy coincidence. There was no story.

Chapter 22.

James Collins lived alone. His wife had died three years earlier and his two children now lived abroad. He spent his days as he had more or less every day since his retirement ten years earlier.

He woke at 7 am, ate a light breakfast and then walked the half mile to the local newsagents, where he bought a copy of the Daily Telegraph. He then walked home, made himself a cup of tea, read the paper pretty much from cover to cover, did the crossword - which usually took him less than an hour - and then he did whatever housework there was to be done.

This was followed by a light lunch and then it was time to open his computer, check his email and perhaps read the BBC website, before dinner and a little TV.

He then retired to bed and read before he switched off his light at about 11 pm. This routine was only broken on Monday when he went shopping in the afternoon, on Friday evening when he attended a local history society and on Sunday afternoon when he went to visit his wife's grave.

So, as this was a Tuesday, James Collins opened his computer as normal at a few minutes before 2 pm. But there was nothing normal about what was waiting for him when he did.

First, he noticed he had 35 emails. Even including spam, he'd never seen the number of emails in double figures before. Perhaps his anti-spam filter was malfunctioning and he was receiving a pile of junk mail.

Collins didn't know much about computers so he hoped there wasn't a problem otherwise he'd have to call in the local computer repairman who regularly fleeced the old man to carry out routine tasks which he could easily manage himself if anyone had bothered to show him.

But when he opened his mail-client he saw the emails were all addressed to him. The other similarity the emails had in common was they were all highly abusive, accusing him of racial hatred, threatening him with violence and one even amounted to a death threat.

James Collins gasped. His heart was pounding and he felt dizzy.

'There must be some sort of mistake,' he thought as he sat back in his chair, closed his eyes and tried to control his breathing. 'Why was he receiving such vile messages, and from people he didn't know?'

Collins was confused and had no idea what to do about it.

'Should he delete the mail and hope it was a virus or something? Should he tell his son? Should he call the police? Did these people know where he lived? Could they really do the things they were threatening? Would they?' The questions flooded into his mind.

Collins sat in silence, breathing rapidly as he struggled to come to terms with the contents of his inbox.

His thoughts were interrupted a few minutes later as the new mail notification pinged and another mail dropped into his inbox. Then another. And another. America was waking up and adding to the torrent of venom pouring out through Collins's computer screen.

Collins decided he needed to read the mail properly to try to discover why he was receiving them and who they were coming from.   So, he took a deep breath and began to read them all, struggling to keep up with the mail which kept arriving as he read.

Most of them accused him of anti-Muslim sentiments, some referred to claims he'd allegedly made that mosques in the UK should be closed down with the religion effectively outlawed, and others were just abusive.

One or two praised him for having the guts to say what he'd said and to have published his email address as a way of being open and transparent about his views.   That was a double-edged sword. He wasn't sure he wanted praise of any kind in this context.

Collins had read enough.   He'd also heard that ping enough so he turned off the notifications, and pushed his chair away from the computer.   He was still confused.   There had to be a logical explanation for all this.   But he couldn't for the life of him think what it could be.

Collins had learned something from trawling through the vile, vicious, venomous outpourings.   He had learned that he was being accused of making outrageous claims and issuing intolerable threats against Muslims.

He didn't know where he was alleged to have made these claims, or when, but there were more than 100 people who had been compelled by them to write to him.

It appeared that wherever he was accused of writing this stuff he had also included his email address instead of hiding behind a pseudonym as so many people did when taking advantage of the internet to say things they would not say in person or behave in a way that would be unthinkable anywhere else.

But the thing which was troubling him most was that he hadn't written anything.   Nor had he said any of the things he was accused of saying.

True, he was concerned about the number of immigrants in the UK, a view which was reinforced daily by his choice of newspaper, but he didn't believe insults, or violence, were the answer.

He was genuinely shocked by the contents of the emails, and the things he was accused of saying. But he had no idea what to do about it. And when he didn't know what to do, over the years he'd found the best thing to do was nothing.

So, he shut his computer, shut his eyes, and tried to shut out the voices in his head which were repeating the contents of the emails in a never-ending loop.

Chapter 23.

Porky lay in bed nervously. He was waiting for them to come for him. It was not the first time he had received a visit at night, and it almost certainly wouldn't be the last. But it was still not a pleasant experience, and however often it happened, you never really got used to it.

Tonight, he knew he was not the only one, which made the atmosphere a little different. He was as prepared as he could be but he was still apprehensive, and, if he was honest at least with himself, a little frightened.

It was going to hurt, perhaps only for an hour, and then it would be over, but the waiting was almost worse than the event.

He scratched his leg and was reminded of the two pairs of swimming trunks he was wearing under his pyjamas. He wasn't entirely convinced it made any difference, but it was the convention and when you tried to get through school unnoticed, you didn't fight convention.

As he waited his turn, Porky reflected on how he'd found himself in this position this time. Three days earlier had been Tottie's birthday, and because he loved being the centre of attention, this was accordingly a big deal. It was mentioned for at least a month beforehand and the day itself was suitably unbearable for everyone. But usually, it was really just a self-indulgent distraction from the routine of school life.

This year, however, had been different. Stevo had had the sycophantic brainwave that everyone, well all eight members of their dorm, should celebrate Tottie getting another year older.

He'd suggested the best way to do this was for everyone to do a 'midnight run'.

In reality, this meant a run at about 10 pm. But the messy bit was that everyone would have to sneak out, run through the nearby park and get back into the dorm without being seen. Not only not being seen by the prefects and housemasters who would still be up and about at that time, but also by any member of the public who might be concerned about seeing a group of teenage boys running through a park at night, then seemingly breaking into one of the school boarding houses. Although in fairness, they had all done it before and they had got away with it without anyone getting caught.

Porky remembered holding his breath in case anyone suggested they modify the plan and go one at a time.

Admittedly, this would have reduced the chances of getting caught because there would not be a large, noticeable, and therefore, noisy group making its way through a deserted park. But it would prolong the activity by eight times as each of them made the 5-minute circuit.

And more dangerously, it would make those who had already done the trip less cautious about keeping the noise down in the dorm until everyone was back.

On balance, all-for-one and one-for-all was a better approach for risky escapades like this.

"OK, that's a good idea," said Nicho. "But..."

Porky's heart sank. Here it was. The moron felt obliged to go one better in his quest for Tottie's admiration. He was going to suggest the relay version, with him, Stevo and Tottie going second, third and fourth, of course.

Some dispensable idiot like Porky would be made to go first, in case it became too risky and then the whole thing could be called off. But not last, for the reasons Porky had already considered.

"But," Nicho repeated. "Why don't we make it a bit better than last time."

'Better' usually meant 'more stupid' in Nicho's head,' thought Porky.

"Why don't we celebrate when we get back by drinking a toast to Tottie."

Nicho looked expectantly at Tottie, desperate for the admiration which he felt his idea so richly deserved.

Porky waited. He was not expected to comment on whether this plan was good, bad or indifferent. That was Tottie's call.

"Good one, Nicho", said Tottie. And that sealed the deal.

Porky reflected on whether the addition of the drink was better or worse than the relay modification. He wasn't sure, but it certainly upped the risk factor as they would have to get away with two breaches of the rules on one evening, both high tariff offences.

Porky was not alone in his apprehension about the birthday celebration. A few of the others clearly also thought it was more reckless than usual, but no-one said anything.

Porky had consoled himself with thinking that Tottie's birthday was still a week away. They still had to buy eight cans of beer and hide them somewhere. Then if it was pouring down on the night, it would almost certainly be called off as too risky even for them.

There was plenty of time for the plan to be changed, but it wouldn't be changed because of a challenge by any of them. The best hope was probably that Tottie would 'chicken out' and find a reason why he'd rather celebrate his birthday another way.

But the day came and Tottie did not have a change of heart, so none of the others could show their reservations either. The plan would go ahead, albeit with a slight, and ultimately, costly amendment.

Porky wasn't sure why the plan had been changed, perhaps it was a slight case of cold feet, perhaps one-upmanship, but whatever the reason, Nicho had suggested that they should have the drink before doing the run.

This would mean his proposal was now more important than Stevo's, and it might also create some Dutch Courage for the second half of the birthday celebrations.

'If only we'd all just agreed to buy a card and sign it," thought Porky as the amendment was considered.

Eventually, it had been agreed they'd have a drink first and that way they could also get rid of the cans while they were doing their run.

So, at about 0945 pm on Tottie's birthday, the cans were cracked open and the eight members of the dorm began to slurp them while sitting in bed.

Well, to be absolutely accurate, six of the group had begun to drink them. This was because Degs, who had been nominated to buy the cans, had opted for a supermarket purchase rather than using the local 'offie'.

He thought this might be less problematic and he was less likely to be challenged by another teenager on the till than he was by the more street-wise owner of the local off-licence. He might have been right but he'd fallen foul of the supermarket practice of bundling.

He could only buy the cans in sixes. He didn't have enough money for 12 cans and, as he was one of those with reservations about the plan, he was reluctant to buy more drink than they needed. This would either encourage someone to drink two or they'd have the problem of trying to hide 4 cans somewhere.

So, much to the dismay of the terrible trio - Tottie, Stevo and Nicho - he'd come back with only six cans. Therefore, the plan was that they'd pass round the cans so they all drank from the six cans in turn.

As far as Porky was concerned, this was not necessarily a bad thing and it enabled everyone to drink as much, or as little, as they wanted before passing on the can to the occupant of the next bed, rather than everyone being obliged to finish an entire can themselves.

All eight would never admit it, but beer had still not become an acquired taste and so drinking a full can was not exactly the most pleasurable experience for any of them.

And so, the cans had been passed around, until they were all finished. It had taken much longer than anyone had expected - about 45 minutes. This was mainly because everyone, apart from Nicho, was sipping rather than swigging, and feigning drinking rather than taking an equal share.

Nicho, of course, was guzzling the beer and by the time the cans were finished, it was fair to say, Nicho was largely responsible for the whole thing not taking more than an hour. As a result, he was acting more stupidly than usual.

Noisy at the best of times, his volume control seemed to have become stuck at least a couple of notches above normal. It was certainly way too loud for 1030 pm, which was about the time the prefects and housemasters started to go to bed, and so they were far more likely to be in the corridors near the dorms, or worse, entering the dorms to go to bed.

The delay in completing the cans had effectively put the second half of the evening in doubt, even in the minds of Tottie and Stevo. The others had never been that keen on attempting the run anyway. Nicho, on the other hand, was well up for it and began cajoling and bullying the others to 'man-up', accusing them of spoiling Tottie's birthday, something even Tottie assured them was not happening.

In the end, it had all become academic as Nicho's increased noise level, coupled with the prefects' bedtime, meant it was inevitable someone would come into the dorm. And they did. And, surprise, surprise they smelled the beer and saw the cans. It was game over.

They weren't going anywhere that night, or anywhere for the next two weeks, it transpired, as the following morning they were all 'gated' which meant they were not allowed to leave the house, other than to attend school.

Furthermore, they were subsequently sentenced to be caned. And that element of the punishment was due to be meted out that evening, which was why Porky, and the others, were lying in bed waiting their turn.

Porky's recalling the events which led up to this evening was abruptly halted as the dorm door opened, and Poppy entered, trying to walk normally, and trying even harder not to speak with tears in his voice.

"Your turn Porky," he said, with as strong a voice as he could manage.

"How was it?" asked Degs, who had not yet made the long walk of pain.

"Ok" was all Poppy could manage before painfully slipping into bed and making sure he did not lay on his back.

No-one asked to see the red marks across his backside, which was the usual practice when someone returned from a caning. For some reason, when everyone was being punished this never happened. Everyone just went back to bed, gritted their teeth and tried not to let anyone know how much it hurt.

Porky slowly got out of bed and began the long walk across the dorm, down two flights of stairs and into the housemaster's study. There, he suspected, there would be little, or no, conversation.

The events of the birthday night had already been established, guilt admitted and sentencing carried out. All that was left was for four strokes of the cane to be administered to the rear ends of the eight miscreants and schoolboy justice would have been done.

Porky took a deep breath, knocked on the door, and cursed Stevo for feeling obliged to come up with something to celebrate Tottie's birthday, Tottie for being the sort of person Stevo wanted to impress; and Nicho for being an idiot. Without them, he would not be answering the voice barking "Enter" which had emerged from behind the study door.

'Why did he have to share a dorm with them? Why did they have to exist?'

Porky turned the door handle and walked to his fate.

Chapter 24.

James Collins was relatively pleased with the way he'd coped over the last five days. He'd avoided the embarrassment of telling his son or calling in the village computer expert to help him out. He'd decided there was no need to alert the police as the threats were effectively anonymous and unlikely to be carried out. That also avoided any unnecessary gossip or rumours in the village.

James Collins knew all too well that rumours did not have to be true, or even be based on truth, for them to spread like wildfire, and last forever. He liked living in the village and as he entered his twilight years, he could certainly live without any 'hassle' - he understood that was modern parlance for kerfuffle.

He had done a little more digging around online and now believed he had found all the blogs, forums and websites where 'his' comments had been posted. He'd noted with interest that the original posts had in fact been well argued, intelligent and reasonable. But a couple of weeks ago, they'd become irrational, offensive and far from well argued. It was this switch in tone that had prompted the hate mail.

Collins wondered if it was the work of two different writers - one a reasonable historian like himself, or even a theologian; and the other a racist agitator. He had changed his passwords to prevent anyone using his accounts or details to post any more of the vile, racist abuse which it appeared he had been posting online. He had opened a new email account and notified the few people who ever emailed him of the new address. He'd told them the old one had been hacked and corrupted so he was starting afresh. He had not opened his old account again so had no idea if the mail had stopped but 'out of sight, out of mind' was working and he felt his life slowly returning to normal.

Collins poured himself another cup of tea, as he looked out over his carefully tended back garden and reflected on how much the incident had shaken him. He had actually had panic attacks, difficulty breathing and cold sweats as he thought about the degree of venom in the mail - mail directed at him personally. He'd never experienced such nastiness and certainly didn't want to have to cope with it ever again.

He took a long drink of his tea and switched on his computer for his daily email check. Collins nearly choked on the tea which he had not yet swallowed. There had to be some sort of mistake. He must have opened his old email account by mistake. He felt a bead of sweat run down his neck and his breathing became erratic. No, it was his new email account and it was showing 300 unread emails.

'Stay calm,' Collins said to himself. 'It might just be a random spam attack, with emails offering him discount viagra, PPI checks, cheap watches or unmissable opportunities to send money to Nigeria to help a potential millionaire claim their vast inheritance, of which 50% would be his on receipt of $50.'

He took a deep breath. It had started again. All as vile as before and all accusing him of racist attacks on Muslims, referring to comments 'he' had posted within the last 24 hours, using his new email address and real name. Collins stared blankly at the screen.

'What now?' 'What should he do?' he thought in a panic.

But his thoughts were interrupted by a loud crash. The sound of breaking glass and a thud. It sounded like the sound was in his front room. Then there was banging on his front door, three very loud thumps on the wooden door.

Collins felt his heart start to pound, all his anxiety attacks returning twice as powerfully as before. His home was being attacked. They'd found out where he lived and were here to kill him, as many of the emails had threatened. Three more bangs on the door. Collins remained frozen in his chair.

"Mr Collins. Mr Collins. Are you home?" called a voice. There was no mistake. They knew his name, and his address and were here for him.

'How would he be able to reason with a lynch mob?' It was time for the police now, but the nearest station was 10 miles away. He could be dead by the time they responded to his call unless there was a patrol car nearby.

Collins's mind raced and he looked around for the house phone to make the 999 call. It was on the other chair. He got up to get it.

"Mr Collins. Are you in?" came the voice again, together with three more loud bangs on the door.

Suddenly things cleared in Collins's brain. 'Mr Collins?' Surely lynch mobs didn't call their victims 'Mr' and why question if he was in? Why hadn't they just smashed down the door?

Collins slowly became more rational and cautiously looked towards the front door. He quietly walked towards the spy hole and looked outside.

Collins breathed again. The first proper breath he'd taken in the last few minutes since he'd looked at his computer. He could see his neighbour and only his neighbour, who was starting to turn away. Collins opened the door.

"Ah you are in," said Danny Waite, Collins's next-door neighbour, turning to face him. He was carrying a box.

"Delivery man left this with me while you were out," he said as Collins remained speechless and ashen on the doorstep.

"Th…..th …anks," he stuttered, taking the parcel from Waite.

"Did you know your bell isn't working," added Waite as he handed it over.

"Er no. Probably the battery," said Collins, regaining some of his composure.

"OK, no problem. See you soon," said Waite, turning to walk back down the short path to the road.

Collins starred after him and realised he was shaking. He turned and went back inside closing the door behind him. As he did, he looked into the front room and there on the floor was a pigeon, its neck was broken, and it was lying in a small pool of blood and pieces of glass. Collins looked at the broken window and let out a deep breath.

He sighed and even managed a slight smile as he realised how nervous he'd become. A pigeon executes a kamikaze mission by flying into his front window and a neighbour delivering a parcel, knocks on his door because his doorbell isn't working, and he was seconds away from ringing the police.

He shook his head in disbelief and began to pick up the dead pigeon and the broken glass. He had a piece of wood in his shed which would patch up the smashed pane while he arranged for the glazier to come and repair it properly, he thought, as he tidied up the mess.

It took Collins about an hour to tidy the front room, board up the broken window, remove the shards of glass and the dead pigeon, clean up the blood on the carpet, fit new batteries to his doorbell and ring the glazier. It was only then that he remembered the parcel which had been delivered at the centre of the drama. He looked around and saw he'd left it on the hall table when he'd seen the dead pigeon.

Collins picked up the parcel and walked into the kitchen. He had no idea what it might be. He hadn't ordered anything. It wasn't his birthday. He wasn't expecting anything at all.

Puzzled, Collins opened the parcel and then dropped it on the floor, letting out an involuntary noise amounting to the start of a scream. Blood splashed across the kitchen floor tiles as a plastic bag in the parcel burst. Collins stared at the heart surrounded by blood and saw there was a piece of metal sticking out from the messy organ. He stifled an urge to be sick and looked a little closer. Whatever it was it had pierced the heart and was sticking out of both sides of the organ.

Collins bent down and tentatively touched the metal to get a better look. He gasped. It was an emblem on a metal stake. A star and crescent, which even an amateur scholar like Collins immediately recognised as a symbol of Islam. The fact that he also knew it was a symbol which had only relatively recently been adopted as a symbol of Islam, rather than the Ottoman Empire or other middle eastern countries, was of no comfort to him at all. The message was unambiguous. He really was at risk, and that risk was now a whole lot closer.

Chapter 25.

Rupert Burns began the long walk home. He liked walking. He did it all day long, so walking home at the end of his shift seemed natural to him. He wouldn't have it any other way. He certainly didn't fancy parking in town, not with all the restrictions and the cost of car parks.

Rupert smiled at the irony of the thought, as he trudged his way home in the rain. Rupert and his wife were traffic wardens. He hadn't always been a traffic warden, but he had done it for many years now since he failed to keep his family's business afloat. His wife had only taken the job because he'd managed to get her it when she was unemployed.

Rupert thought it was the greatest job in the world because he could enforce the law and didn't even have to try to do any investigation or analysis. Power without responsibility. What could be better? His wife only did it for the money and longed to find a 'proper job'.

'The vehicle is either in breach of a regulation, or it isn't,' Rupert infuriatingly loved to point out to anyone who would listen. In truth, he'd have preferred to have been a policeman, but the fairly low standards required were nevertheless a little above his intellect. Of course, he would never have admitted that to anyone, claiming the vigilance required for his role far outstripped that required to be a police officer.

'Furthermore, he was keeping the streets safe and clear of obstruction, while his presence deterred crime,' he contended. But secretly he'd have welcomed the additional powers, most notably the power of arrest, that being a police officer would have brought him.   Then he could have been even more condescending and supercilious to even more people, for even less reason, than he was now.

Rupert usually didn't even consider any other way of getting home, but with the rain lashing down, even his dim-witted brain wondered if driving might be more sensible on days like this. And as if to emphasise the point, a car drove past him, splashing the pavement in front of him.   Most of the dirty water missed him. And with that, Rupert dismissed the notion of driving.

'Walking is far superior,' he thought, smiling like a half-wit. It really didn't take much to amuse him.   He was the human equivalent of Pooh Bear - a man of very little brain.

The rest of Rupert's journey home was as uneventful as his life. He'd managed to avoid being splashed by passing cars, or soaked by lorries, but nevertheless, he was drenched by the time he'd walked the three miles to the house he shared with his wife, Di.

"Hi, I'm home," shouted Rupert, stating the bleeding obvious as he was wont to do so often.

"Where's my little sugar plum?" he added.

Di was in the kitchen, which was also patently obvious given she was using the food mixer, the sound from which filled the small house.   Not only had she heard Rupert come in, she'd watched him walk up the path and even waved to him.

She closed her eyes, took a deep breath, and replied: "In the kitchen darling, where I was when I waved at you through the window ten seconds ago."

She knew this would go right over his head and wouldn't trigger the kind of bickering it might spark between most couples. Di had found that talking to Rupert was all about her tone of voice

- just like talking to dogs. He rarely listened properly so as long as the tone sounded sweet and loving, he'd assume the words matched. She regularly did it with sarcasm and he'd never spotted what she was doing, but she had never had the nerve to actually insult him in a lovey-dovey voice, and see if he noticed.

'One day,' she promised herself.

Rupert kissed her on the cheek, still dripping over everything.

"Have you missed me?" he asked.

His wife moved slightly, partly to stop him kissing her again, but mainly so he didn't drip on her again.

"Terribly," she replied. "Now get those wet things off before I have to mop the kitchen."

"Ooh er, missus, you saucy minx," said Rupert, entirely predictably. He was the sort of man who'd mangle any sentence into an innuendo, however inappropriate, or unfunny.

"Hope you don't say that to all the men," he continued, oblivious to how utterly predictable he was.

His wife sighed again, and silently mouthed: 'I should spank your bottom', only a fraction of a second before her dearly beloved said: "I should spank your bottom." And then he did.

"Won't be long, darling," said Rupert, as he started to take off his coat, leaving another trail of water beside the one he'd left as he'd walked from the door to the kitchen.

"I'll just slip into something more comfortable, and be back down in two shakes of a lamb's tail," he continued, as he dumped his coat at the bottom of the stairs and began to walk up them.

"Although why you'd want to shake a lamb's tail and need to be quick about it is anybody's guess," he laughed at a joke he'd made more times than Di had wondered why she'd married him.

Rupert was the living embodiment of Steve Coogan's Alan Partridge character, perhaps crossed with Boycie, from 'Only Fools And Horses'. He was the sort of man who asked what you were drinking by saying: "What's your poison?" And he invariably added the word 'Squire' to that.

On the rare occasion Rupert did drive the couple's sensible small car, he wore backless leather driving gloves. And regardless of the weather, Rupert insisted on changing into one of his driving jumpers before getting behind the wheel. In fact, he kept a spare one in the boot, along with another pair of driving gloves, a foldable shovel, a blanket, a torch and a waterproof jacket in case of emergencies. Although quite what kind of emergency was likely to befall him when he did less than 1000 miles a year, and 400 of those were going to and from their static caravan where they took their holidays twice a year, was a mystery to Di.

Once she'd joked that perhaps he should keep some emergency flares in there too. But before she could deliver the punchline about never knowing when they might get a surprise invitation to a seventies party, Rupert was already seriously considering the addition to his emergency kit. She was a little surprised he hadn't gone ahead with the purchase.

Di watched as Rupert made his way upstairs, humming to himself. She once again reflected on how she'd found herself in this position and consoled herself by acknowledging that Rupert had been a very welcome port in the storm she'd been experiencing at the time. But nevertheless, to continue the nautical metaphor, he was a classic example of how important it was to make sure you really had no option but to 'jump ship' before you did it. She had effectively left her first husband for Rupert. Hard to believe but something Di had to accept every day.

In fairness, at the start he'd been kind, attentive and appealing in a quirky way. She certainly had seen the best in him. But now, there were no two ways about it, she concluded for the umpteenth time. - Rupert really was a knob. But then she'd been brought up to believe that, 'when you make your bed, you lie in it'. And that applied whatever happened to be sharing it with you. This was the biggest rationale as to why she continued to put up with him and his mannerisms, which would even look ludicrous in a seventies sitcom.

Rupert and Di spent the evening much as they spent most evenings. They ate dinner - pork chops, potatoes, peas and carrots followed by rice pudding. It was Thursday so it was always pork chops, potatoes, peas and rice pudding. The second vegetable varied from week to week in what Di took to be what passed for Rupert's devil-may-care attitude towards routine. Perhaps it was his way of allowing her some freedom and the chance to increase her creativity.

They watched the nightly news, which gave Rupert his daily chance to explain how misguided everyone was and how applying some of his unerring common sense would soon have things sorted out - including world poverty, terrorism and what looked like an impending recession. They watched a sitcom which, not surprisingly, Rupert found hilarious. In reality, it was as jaded as him and peddled predictability as if it was a precious commodity.

Their choice of viewing was restricted to the main terrestrial channels because, as Rupert forcefully pointed out, he may share a first name with a media mogul but that was no reason to add to his wealth by subscribing to Sky TV.

Apparently, there was nothing on Sky worth seeing anyway, Rupert assured his wife, despite his having never seen it and her having spent many happy years watching it.

Di didn't argue. She'd also never had the strength, even in the early days of their marriage, to challenge him about how his views on media moguls equated with him reading The Times. Life was just too short.

So it was with some relief that Di's evening stupor was interrupted by Rupert's announcement that he was going to the study to work on his computer, and would she be ok without him.

"Yes, I'll find something to watch on TV, or maybe read a little," she assured him, without drawing attention to the fact that they didn't have a study. They had an unused second bedroom, which was mainly used for storage, apart from an old table and foldable chair which Rupert called his desk.

She also knew Rupert had no work to do. His job did not involve anything to do with computers and she should know because she was now landed with doing the same one. But such was Rupert's low opinion of his wife that it never entered his head that his statement was nonsense and that she might challenge him on it.

Di knew exactly what he was going to do, didn't care, and in fact, often secretly longed for him to decide it was time to do some work on his computer in the evenings.

Rupert went upstairs and switched on the computer. It didn't take him long to access his 'hidden folder', which in reality was simply called 'Projects' and was no more hidden than any other folder, because Rupert had no idea how to hide a folder anyway.

The folder contained his favourite photos, all downloaded from the web. They could be described as mildly pornographic, but only

116

if seeing topless women on a beach could be described as such. The photos, so titillating and shocking to Rupert, would be pretty mundane to most people. They certainly were to Di, who had found the folder fairly early in their marriage, while she still cared what Rupert did with his time.

Most of the photos were of topless women. A few - his very special shots - involved full frontal nudity, something Rupert found offensive on TV and he had written numerous letters of complaint on the subject. But secretly he enjoyed looking at them. He justified this contradiction by taking the stance that those sorts of images weren't suitable for Di, despite her regularly seeing something uncannily similar in the bathroom mirror after her morning shower.

And so another day in the Burns household drew to a close. Both Rupert and Di were exercising their minds. Di was once again enjoying her day as she had been before Rupert arrived home, watching a documentary on Havana and Cuban music. Rupert was exercising his, by watching what amounted to an online version of the old naturist magazine 'Health and Efficiency', but in colour.

Soon, it would be time for them both to lie on the bed that Di had made for herself, but before that, they both had about an hour or so of relaxation to enjoy. Di was certainly going to take advantage of hers.

But unknown to Di, things were not going as 'swimmingly', as Rupert would say, in the 'study', as they were in the living room. Rupert had followed his usual pattern, largely because he had never deviated from a pattern in his life - that's what patterns were for.

He'd opened the folder and began looking at the photos in his preferred order. He'd then opened Projects 2, which contained very similar images to Projects 1, but this one included a few snatched photos of Di. Photos he'd managed to take when she was getting changed, or coming out of the bathroom without her towel fully covering her body.

Again, there was nothing offensive about them, and although Di had been a little alarmed when she found the photos, it was not because of the content, it was the number of them. She'd been aware of him taking some of them, and if she was honest, when she first suspected that was what he was doing, she had been a little flattered. But that was in the early days.

Later, when he was pointing his phone at her while trying to open an app in that clumsy way he had when he was trying to do anything surreptitiously, he just looked a sad little man and she invariably just sighed and adjusted her towel accordingly.

'He wasn't doing any harm and if it kept him amused,' she concluded, as if dealing with a naughty child.

Rupert did enjoy looking at the photos of his wife, mainly because they were 'naughty' and she wasn't big on walking around naked so getting as many shots as he had was a source of pride to him. He slowly clicked through them and recalled the moment he took each one.

Suddenly, a photo popped up that he could not remember taking. It was of Di, or at least he was fairly sure it was of Di. But unlike the ones he normally took, this one did not include her head. And more surprisingly, this one looked like she was posing. She'd never posed for any photos like this. He'd had to use what he imagined was his ingenuity to get the shots he'd taken. This one was more explicit and he had definitely not taken it.

Rupert couldn't deny he was a little excited by the photo but he was far more perplexed. This photo had not been here last week when he'd last done some work in the study. He would certainly have remembered it. How had it got here?

Rupert's mind began to whirl. He felt a little faint too as the questions came flooding into his head. He hadn't taken the photo, so who had? Was it really of Di, or of a woman who looked a little like her? There was no head so were the other parts of her body distinct enough to identify her? Where had it been taken?

He could not make out anything in the background which was recognisable because it was so dark. Was it a room in this house? Rupert couldn't tell. Was it even inside, or outside? How had it got into his 'hidden' folder? Who had put it there? If someone had put it there, how did they know about the secret folder? Could it have got there by accident? Had he ever seen any photos similar to that one which he might have accidentally saved to the folder last time he was in the study browsing the internet?

But the biggest question of all - what should he do about it?

'What could he do about it?' thought Rupert. He couldn't mention it to Di without revealing his secret stash of photos and the details of his study work. Should he just ignore it? No, he couldn't do that. But he couldn't mention it to her, or anyone else either.

Rupert decided he should sleep on it, or try to, and see if he could decide what to do in the morning. He switched off the computer and walked to the bedroom, deep in thought, which was an unusual state of being for Rupert.

Di was already pretending to be asleep, as she usually did when Rupert had been working in his study. She was expecting him to crash around the bedroom, getting undressed, perhaps coughing a couple of times, before going to the bathroom, and returning as noisily as he'd left, in the hope she'd wake up. She never did, which prompted him to tell anyone who'd listen that 'there could be an earthquake and Di wouldn't hear it'.

But tonight Rupert was unnaturally quiet. He followed his nightly routine, got into bed, switched off the light and went to sleep. Well, he lay silently with thoughts churning around in his head and prepared for what would doubtless be a restless night. Di sighed contentedly.

'Result' she thought and went to sleep almost immediately.

Chapter 26.

James Collins was spared the decision of whether he wanted the shame and distress of calling the police. They called him. In fact, two officers banged on his door less than 10 minutes after Collins found the bird and the gruesome delivery which accompanied it. They were investigating a series of complaints of hate crimes committed by Collins and didn't seem anywhere near as interested in Collins's unwanted and menacing delivery, or his broken window.

The conversation was remarkably quick. Once they had established Collins's identity, verified his email address, and asked him if he knew anything about articles, he had posted which contained offensive comments about Muslims, they formally cautioned him and asked him and his computer to accompany them to the local police station.

Collins was in shock and was again struggling to breathe. He was confused and yet felt guilty and ashamed that the police even considered he'd do such a thing. It was against all his values, his beliefs, his upbringing, everything he stood for his entire life. And now it was being questioned. More than that, it was being demolished. Collins knew his village operated on a no smoke, no fire policy and even if he managed to explain all this and avoid charges, the damage would be done.

As he got into the back of the police car the sad old man saw at least three people watching the drama, a woman pushing a buggy, his neighbour from behind a curtain and the driver of the charity car which picked up people who were not able to travel into the village for doctor's appointments or prescription pickups.

Collins sighed audibly. That was a triumvirate which would ensure the fastest distribution of news known to humanity. The internet might have the global distribution but nothing travelled faster around a small English village than a mum attending numerous playgroups, a neighbour with a big mouth and a driver who spent the entire day gossiping with old people desperate for news about anyone suffering more misfortune than themselves.

He was finished. He'd have to move. But he simply didn't have the strength. And he didn't even know where to begin to explain what was happening to him. At that moment Collins realised he'd been overtaken by the world. He was no longer able to understand, let alone cope with, the way the world worked.

As the car drove through the village, unnecessarily slowly it seemed to Collins, he looked out of the window and saw everyone he knew. They seemed to be lined up along the kerbside as if waiting for a parade, a parade of which he was the star attraction. Of course, he knew that wasn't possible but it simply confirmed his feeling of overwhelming humiliation and shame.

He did not remember much about his processing in the police station, nor his next interview with two detectives. In truth, he didn't understand much of it, other than they were going to send his computer to a forensics lab and it would take a few days to get the results.

He recalled thinking it was very similar to having a blood test and the consequences of the results were equally daunting. He thought the detectives looked incredulous that he'd just kept saying he had no idea how the comments had been posted in his name, using his email account, mentioning his correct address, and on so many websites and forums.

Of course, he'd denied any part of the vilification, which he actually found nauseating, all the more so because he was accused of uttering the filth that was being read back to him.

He didn't recall anything else, nothing about his being bailed pending further inquiries and the results of the forensics, nothing about his walking down the street, nothing about what must have been a subconscious decision not to go home.

He could just see the river in front of him as he looked down from the old bridge. He felt a tear run down his face, fall over the bridge and into the river below as if showing him the way.

Collins closed his eyes and the world turned black.

Chapter 27.

Lemure sighed deeply and sat back, deflated. He tried to silence the voices in his head which were all screaming at once, and he felt a little nauseous. Doubts vied with questions to dominate his thoughts. Questions came almost too quick to be answered. Doubts wormed their way around his brain, infesting his thoughts, poisoning him with indecision. He shook his head and was conscious of how stiff and tense he was. This was not good.

'Get a grip, and calm down' he said to himself, only adding to the voices in his brain.

But at least this voice was more constructive and on-message than the others. He was not used to this degree of confusion and he didn't like it. But then it wasn't every day his meticulous planning did not go smoothly. And today his plans had gone spectacularly off-piste.

Lemure's computer was open on an online article about the death of a retired history teacher. It was a short article, there were few details, and it was only news because the website was a page of a local newspaper which Lemure had been monitoring for the past couple of weeks. 'Otherwise, who would care?'

Well, surprisingly, Lemure cared. He hadn't expected to. In fact, he hadn't expected to be in a position where he had anything to care about. In truth, he hadn't expected Collins to take his own life. But when you spin the wheel, you have no way of knowing exactly where it will stop.

Lemure controlled almost everything about his own life and was very proficient at controlling almost everything about the lives of those he targeted, but he could not control absolutely everything.   And while that irritated him, he knew it and reluctantly accepted it.

So why was Collins's death affecting him so much? Did he feel sorry for the old man?

'Perhaps, a little'.   But he had been chosen for sound reasons and after all, other people had died and it could be argued Lemure had played more than a bit part in their deaths. At best he'd started a chain of events that would lead towards death, sooner or later. And that's all he'd done with Collins.

No, this was more about Lemure, than Collins. This was more about his actions than the unpredicted actions of the old man. This severe bout of second-guessing and analysis was because Lemure really hadn't expected this scenario to end in death. And he had very little experience of what happened, or how to feel when things did not go as he expected.   This was uncharted territory for Lemure.

He hadn't expected death.   Disgrace, shame, a complete withdrawal from what was left of Collins's social life - yes, that had all been part of the plan and that was how he'd expected this to play out.

But Collins had jumped, not only from a bridge but also unceremoniously to the end of his life, avoiding much of the disgrace and shame that Lemure had created for him to endure. Well, avoiding some of the effects of it, the disgrace within him was clearly devastating, and final.

Lemure thought about what he'd done and how he'd incorrectly predicted it would play out. If Collins had only held his nerve for a few weeks, suffering the internal torment of his disgrace and hiding from the external effects of that disgrace that would have come his way, he'd have emerged on the other side.

The area where he'd retired did not have a significant Islamic community, so revenge attacks would have been highly unlikely. The village doubtless contained people who would have been quick to take the moral high ground, and criticise Collins for his actions, but it also probably contained people with dubious bigoted views, not only about Muslims but other religions, races, nationalities, colours and sexual preferences. Collins's torment would have been mainly self-inflicted, if none the less painful for that, and relatively short.

Lemure had been confident that within a few weeks the police forensic team would have concluded that although the offensive material had originated, and been disseminated, from Collins's computer, it had been done while the computer was being controlled by another machine. He was even more confident that the police would neither be able to work out how it had been done, nor be able to trace anything back to Lemure.

Therefore, they would conclude that Collins had either been an unwitting victim, chosen at random, or he'd been deliberately targeted as the victim. Such was Lemure's low opinion of the police's investigatory powers, he was fairly certain they would conclude it was the former, being unable to find any evidence which explained why Collins had been the latter.

Lemure was comfortable with this kind of uncertainty because it didn't really matter which way it went. Collins would have been cleared, faced no charges, and nothing would have been traced back to Lemure.

Of course, Collins would have had to live with his period of disgrace, would never have been completely without blemish in the small community in which he lived but everything would have moved on, leaving 'mission accomplished'.

But that's not how it had ended. Well, not exactly. It was certainly 'mission accomplished', perhaps more than accomplished, but still, it was done.

Collins's family would learn of his innocence soon enough, and perhaps they'd even think more highly of him given his principled action when his integrity had been attacked. Lemure would not be implicated in any way and the operation would move on to the next phase.

'Did Collins's death change anything? Did the operation move on?' Lemure thought to himself.

But even as these questions were forming in his head the answers were crystal clear and he felt himself relax for the first time since he'd read about Collins's death and began to suffer, what to him, was a form of self-doubt.

'Of course, nothing changed. Of course, the operation continued' he answered himself instantly, with absolute clarity and conviction.

'But were there lessons to be learned? Should he make any adjustments because of Collins's premature death?'

Lemure pondered this a little longer. Almost as quickly as a commuter program, he ran through the options and likely scenarios. In little more than a minute he had a decision. He concluded the only thing he could have done, and would do in future, was to improve his assessment of the mental health of his targets, especially if they were going to be pushed close to the edge.

He had checked Collins's email, his medical records, bank balances, anything which could have shown that he was a potential suicide risk, and he had discounted it. That was clearly a mistake and Lemure did not make mistakes.

In future, he'd monitor things a little more closely, travelling to the scene, if necessary, to make sure things went the way he planned, not the way fate dictated.

He was in control of this operation, not destiny with faulty dice. It would increase the risk slightly if he was seen and he might have to create a false alibi to place him elsewhere to cover that. But given he had no intention of ever being seen or linked to any of his victims, it seemed a minor risk and one worth taking if it prevented any more unforeseen events.

Lemure hated 'unforeseen'. It was so amateur. Everything could be foreseen, predicted, monitored and delivered as envisaged. Anything less was a failure. This had been a failure. There would not be another one.

At that, the voices in Lemure's head fell silent. He replaced the silence by pressing the remote and filling his head, his room and his life, with music. He was back on track.

Chapter 28.

Rupert Burns was having a nightmare day, to follow his nightmare night. He'd slept badly, had woken repeatedly, and then was sound asleep when the alarm went off at 7 am.

Di was on shift with him that day so they'd both got up, showered, had breakfast and left the house together. They drove to work, as Di insisted they did when they were on shift together. The atmosphere was strained, so much so, that Di had asked Rupert if he was OK. For a second, he'd considered answering truthfully and telling her, but what would he say? Instead, he'd assured her he was fine.

"Just a bit of a headache," he lied. "Probably shouldn't have spent as long staring at that computer screen last night," he added, more truthfully.

The day had dragged and for the first time he could remember, Rupert's heart really wasn't in dishing out tickets - deserved or not. He walked his beat, gave out the most obvious tickets, but passed over even more offences and didn't get close to his normal practice of actually looking for lawbreakers.

He had taken his lunch in a park on his round to avoid having to eat with Di. He still did not know how to tackle the subject of last night's revelation.

'Was she having an affair?' he thought, for the first time in their marriage, conveniently ignoring the fact that they had had an affair while Di was still married to her former husband, although perhaps subconsciously knowing she was therefore capable of it.

But even if she was, that didn't explain the photo turning up on his computer. Perhaps to avoid the reality of what had happened Rupert was increasingly coming to the conclusion the photo was not of his wife. He began to convince himself the woman in the photo had bigger breasts, darker nipples, less pubic hair, anything that would make it less likely to be his wife.

'So, if it isn't her,' he concluded, 'then most of his problems went away.'

The only remaining issue was how a photo he had neither taken, nor knowingly downloaded, had got into his private collection. He pushed away any doubts he had about this conclusion and began to find explanations for the photo being on his computer.

The most likely theory was he'd downloaded it by accident. Perhaps there was a way a photo could be downloaded without him doing anything, a bit like how other web pages opened as if by magic when he clicked on certain links.

Rupert knew next to nothing about computers which meant he had no idea how to explain what had happened but his ignorance also enabled him to explain the event with the most inexplicable theories and happily convince himself he was right.

Rupert had never had a problem believing his own bullshit, and if the truth be told, he was fairly susceptible to the bullshit of others too.

He managed to get through the rest of the day becoming more and more convinced he'd solved the mystery and more and more pleased he hadn't mentioned anything to Di.

'How embarrassing it would have been to challenge her about something she knew nothing about, and in the process expose the true nature of his nocturnal studies,' he thought.

'What a schoolboy error that would have been?' And for the first time in almost 24 hours, he smiled.

'Shows what a guilty secret can do to your mind,' he reasoned.

All sorts of weird flights of fancy could take place, which could have had catastrophic effects on, not only his guilty pleasure, but also on his marriage and his future.

'Good job he was made of sterner stuff and hadn't lost his nerve. Top man Burns,' he congratulated himself.

But Rupert resolved to take another closer look at that photo tonight, just to check out those physical discrepancies, which he'd convinced himself were considerable and would prove it wasn't Di.

Di met Rupert outside the council offices at the end of their shifts, as arranged.

"Where were you at lunchtime?" she asked as soon as he arrived. "I waited for you but then had lunch with Steph and Amanda instead."

Rupert hated Steph, which was why Di had mentioned her. But he didn't react.

"Sorry sugar plum," he replied, "Lost track of time and would not have made it back on time. I sent a text. Didn't you get it?" he

"No, I didn't," said Di, checking her phone, knowing full well he was lying but going through the motions of checking as she so often did to make him think she swallowed his lies.

In truth, she'd preferred lunch with her friends and hadn't tried too hard to find Rupert, but that was no reason not to make the point, especially after Rupert's strange behaviour that morning.

'Still, he was now acting far more like his normal self,' she thought. 'Unfortunately'.

The couple drove home and, by the time they got there, Di decided things were back to normal and she began to simply tolerate him again.

Their evening followed the usual pattern, almost identical to the previous evening, except today being Friday and the end of the working week for both of them, it was takeaway fish and chips for dinner, which they'd picked up on their way home.

But then Rupert did surprise her a little, by again announcing he had to finish off some work he hadn't had time to do the previous night. It was very unusual for Rupert to escape to his study two nights running, but Di was more relieved than annoyed by his change of habit.

Once inside the study, with the door not only closed but wedged with a folder he'd placed behind it to give himself some warning if Di decided to barge in. Not that she ever had but he couldn't take the risk at such a crucial point.

Rupert switched on the computer and immediately opened the second Projects folder. He scrolled through the photos until he found the rogue snap.

'Please let it be a different woman,' he thought as he clicked on the image to inspect it in closer detail.

But instead of the screen being filled with naked flesh, belonging to his wife or otherwise, the screen flashed white. Then the white began to disappear into a hole in the middle of the screen, like a white sheet being pulled out of the back of the computer, leaving Rupert staring at a black screen.

Rupert repeatedly clicked the enter key without effect. He pressed control-alt-delete which he'd learned from a geeky bloke down the pub. It was the total extent of his computer knowledge and it had absolutely no effect.

Rupert began to get a little more desperate. He pressed the on-off button. Nothing. He turned off the power. Nothing. He unplugged the power cable as if that was different from turning off the power. Nothing. The machine was dead.

Rupert realised immediately he now had no choice but to mention the computer problem to Di. She occasionally used it for whatever she used it for. Rupert had no idea. But he had to tell her it was broken or she'd find out soon enough.

He then realised tomorrow was Saturday and Rupert usually went for what he invariably called a 'swift snifter' at The Snooty Fox on Saturday evenings. Geeky Andy was always there. He worked with computers. Rupert would ask him what to do. Pay him to take a look at it, if necessary. Then he could get back to sorting out the problem of the mystery photo and get his life back on track. This need not be a major problem, after all, he reasoned.

So perhaps he didn't need to draw Di's attention to the computer, just yet. He'd stay in his study for a little longer, reading, to let her think he was working, then carry on as normal. Tomorrow he'd talk to Geeky Andy and everything would be 'tickety boo'.

Chapter 29.

Saturday in the Burns house was as uneventful as every other day. Rupert spent most of the day with a group of like-minded enthusiasts who shared his obsession with flying model aeroplanes. They flew the irritating machines above an area of parkland which meant everyone walking in the area had an incessant buzzing in their heads like they were being stalked by a swarm of angry wasps.

Di caught up with her household chores, changed the bedding, put on the washing machine and cleaned the bathroom. She then settled down at the computer to do a little online 'window shopping', before going into town to do the weekly grocery shop. And so it was that Di discovered their computer wasn't working. She tried most of the things Rupert had tried the previous evening with as little success.

'That's odd,' she thought. 'It must have been working OK last night or Rupert would have mentioned there was a problem'.

Still, it wasn't a big deal. She was going into town anyway so could drop it off at the computer shop where they advertised repairs at a reasonable price.

The queues at the supermarket were longer than usual, so together with that and having to drop off the computer at the repair shop, Di wasn't home by the time Rupert returned from playing with his planes.

He quickly changed and headed for The Snooty Fox and his intended conversation with Geeky Andy.

Rupert spent a couple of hours in the pub, drank his usual two and a half pints of bitter shandy, and grilled Andy to within an inch of his life about the computer. He didn't mention his photo problem specifically but managed to find out how to actually hide folders, which he intended to do as soon as the computer was repaired. Andy had given him some things to try but had said he would probably need to take a look at it. They had agreed Rupert could drop it off at Andy's place on Sunday if his suggestions didn't sort it out.

So, Rupert was in a better mood than usual when he breezed into the kitchen to find Di preparing dinner. Saturday - that was home-made curry day.

"Hi sugar plum," he said as he walked straight through the kitchen, pausing only to kiss her quickly on the cheek.

"Must dash to the toilet," he said. "Should have gone before I left the 'Snoots'." And he almost ran upstairs without Di having a chance to say a word.

Rupert did go into the toilet and flushed it before nipping into the study to immediately try the suggestions on the computer.

"Darling, where's the computer?" he asked as he came back downstairs, trying to sound as natural as possible.

"Oh, it was dead when I tried to use it earlier, so I took it to the repair shop in town," she replied, without looking up from chopping onions.

"They'll take a look on Monday and let us know what's needed sometime on Tuesday. Don't worry there's no charge for them to take a look, and they will give us an estimate on the cost of any repairs before doing anything," she added to prevent Rupert's careful attitude to money kicking in.

Rupert quickly made a decision, one he might regret but one that seemed the easiest at the time. He'd go along with her assumption that he didn't know about the computer problem.

"What's wrong with it?" he asked. "It was OK last night," he lied.

"It was just dead when I tried to turn it on. I tried all the usual things, turning it on and off etc. but there was just nothing. It was completely dead. The guy at the shop said it might be a lot of things, so he didn't want to guess how much it might cost to repair.

"It could even be something very simple - and cheap," she added, to further allay the possible onset of Rupert's fiscal fury. He really didn't like to spend money on things that did not produce anything material. Repairs were not like buying new things and so they fell into the waste of money category, as far as Rupert was concerned.

Rupert quickly thought through this unexpected development and tried to assess its implications, which when you were as mentally limited as Rupert was actually quite a slow process. So slow, in fact that Di noticed the silence, looked up, and said: "That's OK. Isn't it? I haven't done anything wrong, have I?"

"No, not at all," replied Rupert, not sure if she had or not.

On the plus side the computer shop would definitely work out the problem, whereas there was no guarantee Andy's suggestions would have fixed it, and so it would probably have had to go to him tomorrow anyway.

On the downside, it would probably cost more money to repair than it would have done, even if he'd had to pay Andy.

But the bigger worry that was nagging at him, was the photos. Rupert had read about people getting caught having porn on their computers when they'd been reported by computer repair shops.

'Surely that wouldn't become a problem, would it?' he wondered. 'His photos were well hidden in their secret folders, he rationalised erroneously, 'and they were mainly topless photos and just a few full frontals. There were none depicting even 'normal sex' let alone some of the perversions he sometimes came across while trawling for acceptable images to download.

'OK, there were some of Di, and she was recognisable, which might be embarrassing for her if the guys in the shop saw them and realised they were of her," he realised. 'But that wasn't really a problem, well not for him,' he decided, with his usual degree of selfishness. 'And they were unlikely to mention it to her, probably just share a snigger at her expense - if that.'

"Tell you what, let me know what they say on Tuesday, and I'll pick it up once it's ready," he said, thinking that might at least stop the guys working out some of the images were of Di - if they even found them at all.

"How long until dinner, honey bunch? Have I time for a shower? he asked, now happy that even with the change of plan everything was still going to be 'tickety boo'.

Chapter 30.

Unfortunately for Rupert Burns 'tickety boo' was not at all how the computer technician saw things when he sat down to take a look at the Burns' computer first thing on Monday morning.

He'd plugged it in, turned it on, and despite what the lady had reported as the fault, the computer came to life, almost as normal.

'Almost' as normal, because instead of the standard boot screen turning into the desktop as icons appeared one by one, the screen was instantly filled with the naked image of what appeared to be a teenage girl in a changing room. It was difficult to be sure of her age, but she was certainly younger than 18 and from the angle of the photo, it didn't appear she had the faintest idea she was being photographed. She certainly wasn't posing.

A quick search of the other photos on the computer revealed a large stash of similar images, mostly taken in changing rooms. There were also some more hardcore images, which, while they would not fall into the highest category of illicit pornography, they were certainly obscene, and were way above the topless images Rupert had been concerned about in folders Projects 1 and Projects 2. The contents of Projects 3 required the technician to call the police immediately.

And so Rupert heard about his computer on Monday, rather than Tuesday, but not from Di, or the shop. He received a visit from the police to caution him and take him in for questioning.

After that, things moved very quickly despite Rupert vehemently denying any knowledge of the images the police showed him. He tried explaining how an image he didn't download had appeared on his computer and therefore these had probably arrived the same way.

Unfortunately, apart from being technologically naive and extremely weak, his reasoning was not helped by the fact that the mystery image which he'd been so worried about before the weekend, could now not be found on his computer. Now, he had lots more images to worry about, and these ones carried a jail sentence.

Rupert was charged with a number of counts of possessing indecent images and bailed while the police investigated whether he was also part of a paedophile ring and whether he'd actually taken the voyeuristic photos in what appeared to be the changing rooms of the local sports centre, and a couple of the high street stores.

Actually, the images were of poor quality and so the locations might be difficult to verify, but the police did not share these reservations with Rupert.

Within days Rupert was suspended pending the outcome of the police investigation. The justification for this was that Rupert was employed by the council and, as some of the photos could have been taken on council property, namely the local swimming pool and gym, this would be an abuse of his position.

Within two weeks, Di had moved out and was staying with her mother while she 'took some time to think'.

In reality, she'd done all the thinking she was going to do. After all, surely nobody was expected to lie in this bed, and she certainly hadn't made this one for herself. This gave her the excuse she needed to leave him, something her pride had prevented her from doing since she'd jumped into a rebound marriage after being caught having something of an affair with the half-wit.

Conversations with his lawyer had not gone well either. Rupert gave a very convincing performance of denying knowing anything about the images, how they'd been taken, who'd taken them, where they'd been taken, who the girls were, how old they were, or how the images had ended up on his computer. But claiming to know nothing didn't really amount to any form of defence when the evidence was starkly apparent, and frankly, overwhelming, in amount and nature.

Rupert had been shocked when his lawyer had said that while he may believe Rupert's denials, there was no way a court would accept them and that despite claiming to be innocent, he should consider pleading guilty.

Rupert was outraged and didn't even properly hear his lawyer explaining that he was almost certain to receive some form of prison term if he pleaded not guilty and was then convicted of the charges at trial.

If the police added any charges relating to the taking of the photos, or of distributing them, he was certain to be jailed. However, as the changes stood at present, they were at the lower end of the tariff.

If he pleaded guilty, he'd be put on the sexual offenders' register but he might avoid jail because he had no previous convictions of any sort.

Chapter 31.

Porky made his way through the crowded corridors of the school, as hundreds of his fellow pupils switched rooms between lessons. It was a manic five minutes repeated every forty minutes during the school day, as boys resembling ants crisscrossed their way to the next lesson.

Porky generally enjoyed the school day, it was the hours after school and at weekends that were difficult. As one of the more intelligent boys in his year, Porky was in the top set for all of his subjects, especially now that he'd made his choices for GCSEs. That ensured that he was no longer in any class with his tormentors, who, with the exception of Tottie, were not the brightest of the bunch. Tottie was the most intelligent but he squandered his talents, unless it involved a sport, then he excelled.

Choosing his GCSE subjects had been very straightforward. The school was totally academically focussed and so the groupings of available subjects favoured those boys who wanted to stick with traditional subjects like Latin, Maths or English Literature, and had no need of more modern subjects like Economics or Spanish. However, there was still room for arts and crafts, and this was where Porky had run in to a problem with his choices. He had no real artistic talent and was dextrously challenged in anything that involved fine detail. Art was a non-starter as nothing Porky ever drew bore the remotest resemblance to what it was meant to be. He had realised this inability early in his life. While at primary school his class was tasked with drawing the scene of the Gunpowder Plot, as Guy Fawkes loaded the cellars of the Palace of Westminster with explosives, intending to blow up the House of Lords. Porky realised he couldn't draw people - well not if the intention was for them to look human rather than robotic - but he discovered he could draw a pretty acceptable barrel. So he set about perfecting his barrel drawing. In fact, he got a little carried away and proceeded to fill the paper with barrels, all neatly stacked against the wall. He was actually almost enjoying himself as he'd rarely drawn anything recognisable before. Until the teacher came round and stood behind him, that is.

"That's a lot of barrels you've drawn there," she said. "Where's Guy Fawkes?" she asked, not unreasonably.

"He's just gone out to get another barrel," Porky had replied instantly, without the slightest intention of being a smart arse. It was simply how he'd seen things.

Unfortunately, it was not how the teacher had seen things, and while shouting at him for being cheeky, she'd pointed out how ridiculous his drawing was. From that moment on, Porky knew art was not for him.

Two other choices were woodwork and technical drawing. Neither were really options for Porky. Woodwork involved precision and making pointless things like a dove-tail joint with two pieces of wood. Nobody ever made a table or chairs, or a desk, or anything useful. Not that Porky would have had the technical expertise to make such things, even if he'd been given the option. But toiling away to join two pieces of wood together when a decent nail would do the job in seconds, seemed particularly pointless to him. Technical drawing was just art without the creativity. He had to be even more accurate with his pencil and he lost the thin veil of flexibility provided by what was sometimes called artistic licence.

So Porky was left with only one option - pottery. The last bastion of the non-artistic. At least you could make things which were useful, like a vase or a jug, and it was kind of cool to see how the chemicals changed colour in the kiln. Anyway, pottery was his inevitable selected GCSE choice and that was where he was going now, for a double period of 80 minutes. All art and craft lessons were doubles.

The main problem with pottery was that it not only attracted the non-artistic, it also attracted some of his less intelligent compatriots. The mathematical precision of woodwork and technical drawing simply seemed too difficult for many of the intellectually challenged, so unless they could actually draw, they too opted for pottery. As a result, this provided the only time in the school timetable when Porky had to share a class with all three of his tormentors.

Porky now hated pottery and resented his lack of artistic ability. He was already taking nine other GCSEs and was likely to get good grades so why couldn't he simply drop pottery and just take his nine As into the sixth form? Sadly, things didn't work like that when success was measured so numerically and when so many pupils were high achievers.

So now, Porky faced 80 minutes of misery, unless he could drag out the journey to the pottery room a little longer, but he knew he'd never get rid of more than five to ten minutes by dawdling.

Porky pushed open the door and walked into the large room, filled with work branches, shelves stacked with work in progress and a door through into the kiln room. He took off his jacket and put on his clay-stained apron. After a quick look around the room, he realised the terrible trio were already there and had set up their equipment at the far end of the room, near the large extractor fans.

Porky would have bet good money that's where they would be. They always tried to get at that end of the workroom, which was why he always tried to work at the opposite end, but then so did everyone else. The trio preferred that end of the room because of the proximity to the extractor fans, not because of their intended purpose to keep the air inside fresher than it would otherwise be with the kiln fumes and the chemicals used to stain the pottery. No, they liked the fans because of their sheer mechanics. They had massive metal blades which revolved at speed to move air inside to outside relatively quickly. Just what you'd expect from an industrial extractor fan. The added bonus to Tottie and his doting henchmen was that the fans also moved other things from inside to outside relatively quickly, in particular, clay.

The pottery teacher, Pixie Perkins, so named because he resembled a creature from Tolkien's middle earth, complete with tweed jacket and leather elbows, had a troubling habit of 'nipping out' of most lessons. Nobody knew where he went, nor why he needed to do it every lesson. Other teachers did the same - notably 'Sore Arse' Rawbottom, a maths teacher who couldn't go 40 minutes without a cigarette - but their reasons were usually apparent. Not so with Pixie. He just disappeared at random, and could be gone much longer than a normal fag break. These unexplained absences provided carte blanche for Tottie, Nicho and Stevo to run riot with impunity for a sizeable chunk of the lesson. The breaks wreaked havoc for everyone but they could be mitigated when the fans were on. Tottie and his acolytes loved to throw large lumps off clay around the room, but they especially loved throwing the clay into the huge fans. This had the effect of slicing the clay into small pieces and spraying the brown gunge all over the cars parked on the street outside. Later, the trio would walk past the cars laughing uproariously as the brown spray started to dry into hardening lumps of clay, which took some effort to remove. As far as Porky was concerned, it was a good lesson if they amused themselves lobbing clay intro the fans for the whole duration of Pixie's absence. A bad lesson was when they quickly bored of that, or the fans weren't on. Then, they switched to throwing clay at other members of the class, or tried to lob a massive chunk so it landed on the work of another pupil.

Porky found a space at the far end of the room and went to collect his almost-complete piece of work. It was a distinctly average oblong vase which he'd made with slabs of clay because he'd never mastered the potter's wheel to create a cylindrical one. Average, it undoubtedly was, but for Porky it was probably the best piece of work he'd ever managed to create and it was also relatively useful.

He carried the treasured piece to his workspace and looked with reassurance at Pixie who was unusually sitting at the front of the room sorting through some papers. Perhaps it wasn't the level of hands-on teaching the school would expect but for Pixie this amounted to devoted attention. More importantly for Porky, it amounted to protection. If Pixie was in the room there was a degree of calm and control. If he left, it would descend into mayhem within seconds and then, anything could happen.

Whatever Pixie was sorting, it was keeping him busy, and more importantly, in his very visible seat at the front of the room. In fact, it kept him there for almost an hour which was excellent, and enough for Porky to actually start to relax and to focus on putting the finishing touches to his vase. Soon, it would be ready for firing in the kiln.

And then it happened. Pixie got up, looked at his watch, and left the room. He could only have been out for 15 seconds when the proverbial hit the fan, well a lump of clay to be more accurate. It thudded into the blades and was smashed into dozens of tiny pieces and flung across the road below.

'Don't panic', Porky told himself. 'They have been cooped up for a long time and lobbing lumps of clay into the fan usually keeps them occupied for a while. If this is just a ten-minute window of opportunity then that might be enough to prevent them looking for other distractions.'

And he was right. The mindless potters were very content - and hugely amused - by throwing larger and larger lumps of clay into the fan for more than ten minutes. Unfortunately for everyone else, Pixie clearly believed that his prolonged dedication to paper sorting had earned him a longer break than normal. Ten minutes passed. Then twelve. Still, the morons were amusing themselves. But unlucky thirteen followed as it inevitably does and the fan's spell was broken as quickly as it had been cast.

The room's general hubbub had risen in proportion to the length of tutorial absence, so it was fairly noisy as most people took advance to chat and joke with their class mates. But despite this, and the distance between Porky and the other end of the room, he still clearly heard the words: "Oh look what Porky has made.'

It was Nicho. He rarely spoke quietly and was incapable of whispering, but this was loud enough to cut through the background noise. As the words carried across the room, the class began to quieten. They knew instinctively that something unpleasant was going to happen. Many of them knew that if it was going to happen to Porky, it was less likely to happen to them. All *they had to do was keep their heads down and let whatever was going to happen, happen to Porky and not to them.*

Porky felt the attention of the room start to switch to him. Even those with their heads down were furtively looking at him.

"Oh, that's lovely Porky," continued Stevo. "Mummy will love that. She can put her pansies in it. She likes pansies, doesn't she?'

"Porky is her little flower," picked up Nicho. "Perhaps she will put Porky in the vase."

Inexplicably, this pathetic, meaningless quip really amused Tottie. That was the Holy Grail, amusing Tottie was what they lived for. Tottie laughing at something you'd said was one of the highest accolades Stevo and Nicho could achieve. Nicho beamed at the endorsement of what he assumed was his unrivalled wit. But encouraging the terrible twosome only served to egg them on to more stupidity. Nicho was already thinking as quickly as his brain could process thoughts in a desperate search for something equally funny he could add. Stevo was carrying out a similar fruitless exercise with as little success.

The moment was beginning to die. Nicho was getting more desperate to find his next comment, but he could only think of his last one. So, perhaps it was inevitable that he suddenly blurted out: "Would you like to be in a vase, Porky?"

Porky sighed. This was only going one way. 'Why couldn't Pixie come back into the room and be where he should be for the rest of the lesson?' he thought.

Porky looked at the door, willing it to open. It stayed resolutely closed. Nicho was looking at the door too. But the mental transference of his wishes onto the stationary door was more successful than Porky's.

'How could that work?' thought Porky. 'Nicho barely has enough grey matter to keep himself alive and yet his wish that the door stay closed was clearly far stronger that Porky's increasingly frantic wish that it would open.'

Porky's attention left the uncooperative door and switched to Nicho who was rapidly approaching him. Stevo was only a couple of steps behind.

Porky could clearly see what was about to happen and, as usual, he was powerless to stop it. Before he could even try to stop it, he was grabbed roughly by Nicho. Seconds later, Stevo also grabbed him. Porky struggled - although he didn't know why he bothered. He didn't know why he ever bothered, was it instinct or was he just playing the game and pretending to put up resistance so that his attackers would feel more accomplished when they overcame it? They were both so much stronger than him, and together, there was no chance Porky could break free or even stop them moving him wherever they wanted to move him. He had no doubt where they were moving him to. And with that feeling of inevitability, Porky felt his face smash into the cold, wet clay that had previously formed the carefully created neck of his vase.

"Oh, that's a shame, Porky won't fit in the vase," laughed Nicho.

"And I thought it was especially for pansies," added Stevo, finally managing to link something vaguely related to his earlier jibes.

It was all over in seconds. Once they had pushed Porky's face into the clay, and squashed the unfinished vase in the process, they relaxed their grip and quickly returned to their end of the room, laughing loudly and looking expectantly at Tottie. They were not *disappointed.*   *He was grinning broadly and laughing at the hilarious antics of his henchmen.*

"You might want to nip out for a wash, Porky," said Tottie. "You've managed to get clay all over your face.   It looks like you've been eating it, you idiot.   It's lunch next.   Were you too hungry to wait?"

Nicho and Stevo almost burst at the intellectual humour of their leader and were laughing uncontrollably by the time they got back to their respective workstations, just as the inevitable happened. The door finally yielded to Porky's superior intellect and opened.

"Alright, alright, keep the noise down" said Pixie, as he breezed back into the room totally unaware of what had occupied a section of the room for more than 15 minutes, let alone the last two.

"It's like a zoo in here," he added as he headed back to his desk.

'He's got that right,' thought Porky, as he tried to wipe his face and looked at the crumpled clay in front of him.   A brown blob which had once been the finest piece of art he'd ever made.   It had now returned to a state very similar to the one in which he'd found it weeks earlier - a lump of un-moulded clay.   He now had to recreate it in the week that was left before it had to be handed in for firing and then marked as part of his GCSE submission.   Porky sighed.   He knew where he would be spending most of his evenings this week.

Chapter 32.

Lemure liked to be one step ahead. In fact, one step was the bare minimum. He was often so far ahead of himself that by the time some things came to fruition he'd almost forgotten he'd started them. Not that he ever completely lost touch with his projects, they were just so well planned that most of them ran so smoothly that they required very little intervention.

The secret was in the meticulous planning, which was what took most of his time. In fact, his life was largely about planning. The culmination of the plan was satisfying but, to Lemure, it was really only confirmation of what he knew was going to happen.

That was why the Collins 'glitch' had affected him so deeply, and still was affecting him, weeks later. The memory kept coming back to him, however much he rationalised that there had been nothing he could have done differently.

But he was now getting ready for what was likely to be the final countdown. The end-game. And although it would require just as much planning, it would require far more action, far more involvement, and that both excited and concerned Lemure.

There could not be any trace, this time. This time the police were likely to become far more involved. And, stupid as they were in Lemure's opinion, careless loose ends were likely to be spotted if enough people were looking for them.

'What was that story which was quoted as an example of the definition of infinity?' thought Lemure, as he worked at his computer.

'That's it - give an infinite number of monkeys an infinite number of typewriters and they will eventually write all the great works of Shakespeare. Well give an infinite number of police an infinite amount of time and they will eventually find a loose-end which could solve a crime', thought Lemure, smiling to himself.

'Either that or they'd make one of their 'breakthroughs' because a member of the public would eventually contact them and tell them who was responsible.'

Well, Lemure was going to make sure neither of those scenarios was going to happen. He wouldn't be leaving any loose ends and nobody knew anything about what he did, or how he did it. He never involved anyone else in his work. He never discussed it. He never wrote about it. He never had and he never would. And he destroyed everything which could incriminate him as soon as he no longer needed it.

Lemure returned his focus to the webpage he was reading. He was researching a subject he'd partially researched before. He'd never actually experimented with it as fully as he'd wished, but it fascinated him, as it had fascinated people for centuries. That was why there was so much to research online, and so many examples all around him. He'd never realised nature was so dangerous.

'How on earth did people ever work out what was safe to eat?' he wondered. 'I suppose they didn't. They just died when they got it wrong but if starvation was the alternative, then eventually a society would work out what was safe, and what wasn't.'

Lemure was researching what wasn't. He read:

All parts of the hemlock plant are poisonous. The effects are a weakening of the muscles with intensive pain which can begin in less than 30 minutes, although it can take hours to die.

Lemure could understand why it was the poison of choice through the ages, as was the next one - Arsenic.

Arsenic is an element, usually found as a white powder which has to be swallowed. It causes severe damage to the stomach and creates great pain. Given in a large dose, traces would be found in the digestive tract. Administered in small doses, over a period of time, the element would be found in the victim's hair or fingernails. There are a number of tests which can detect arsenic poisoning.

'How science moves on,' thought Lemure. 'No longer the undetectable remedy for a meddling king, or emperor from history.'

He read on, finding some more unexpected killers.

All parts of the flowering shrub Oleander are deadly. It is similar to Digitalis, in that it over stimulates the heart and the effects are immediate. Azaleas and Rhododendrons are poisonous with the effects starting within six to eight hours. The poison causes vomiting, low blood pressure, seizures and coma.

'Sounds very messy,' thought Lemure. 'That would take a lot of clearing up. Ahh, cyanide.'

There are a number of forms of cyanide, some of which have industrial uses. Others occur naturally in some seeds and fruit stones, like hydrocyanic acid, which can be found in the stones of peaches, apricots or plums, among others. Cyanide can be swallowed, inhaled, or absorbed through the skin. It causes asphyxiation by damaging the body's cells, which prevents them from absorbing oxygen. The effects are instant and death can occur within 15 to 30 minutes.

Here was the bit that Lemure was familiar with, and was often mentioned in crime novels.

During a post-mortem, a bitter almond smell can be detected.

And another old favourite:

Strychnine is not as quick to act as arsenic or cyanide and it has a bitter taste. The effects start to develop in less than half an hour and include spasms and convulsions. Death is usually caused by asphyxiation.

Lemure shook his head. Strychnine was popular with novelists but less common in the real world of killers, as it was so easily detected. Now here were some more unusual toxins. Lemure read on.

Methanol is distilled and found in perfumes, anti-freeze and paint removers. If swallowed, it metabolises into formaldehyde in the body. This causes severe abdominal pain, vomiting, and difficulty breathing. Death is usually caused by respiratory failure. Symptoms do not normally manifest for up to 24 hours, by which time it is too late to save the victim. A victim must get treatment within a couple of hours of swallowing the methanol.

Lemure was growing impatient. Admittedly he was learning and was interested in his subject but most things seemed too chemical, and not natural enough. 'What about things that grow in the wild, or ….? Ah, reptiles.'

There are many different types of poisonous reptiles, and most of them require different antidotes. Within 30 minutes, venom from adders can cause vomiting of blood, loss of vision and collapse can occur within the hour. The venom from cobras paralyses the nervous system. Symptoms begin within minutes and, like adder venom, death can occur within a couple of hours, if no antidote is administered.

'Suppose that was similar to the venom from the stonefish which killed David Stevenson last year,' thought Lemure. 'We could go full circle. There was a nice symmetry about that.'

Toxic mushrooms are common and vary considerably in colour, including the most well publicised, red with white spots. The toxin affects the liver, kidney and heart muscles with symptoms slow to develop. It can take as long as 48 hours for the victim to experience any symptoms, which include violent stomach pains and vomiting, but the damage to the liver can be so severe that a transplant can be the only effective treatment.

Lemure had read enough for one evening. He closed the computer, his search history deleting automatically. Not that it could ever be traced, given the amount of security between him and the internet, but it was part of his routine, and routine was important.

He turned on some music and flicked through the options. He quickly settled on the largely instrumental Pink Floyd album, 'The Endless River'. He didn't need any more words. He needed calm and to relax before bed. It was essential his mind stayed focussed and to do that it needed regular periods of relaxation. He still had a lot of work ahead of him in the next few weeks.

Chapter 33.

Brian Tottingham had one eye on his dealing screens and one on the clock. It had been a long week and it was only Thursday. But at least the markets were about to close for the day and Brian could head home, after a couple of drinks in the local wine bar, of course.

After leaving school, Brian had managed to create a lucrative career for himself by falling into a job as a runner at one of the big dealing houses. His knack for maths had helped his career progress but not nearly as much as his market-trader, cheeky-chappie approach. He had found his ideal macho world, where being a chancer was rewarded - handsomely.

Brian, like most people who worked in an industry that had seen more lucrative times, believed he'd missed the gravy train and was cursed not to have been born 10 years earlier when market traders were dripping in gold.

But in fact, Brian was still on the gravy train, perhaps one of the last few carriages, and it may not have been as rich as it once was, but it had served him well over the 15 years he'd worked in finance. He wasn't in the category of private yachts or jets, but his salary, and more particularly, his bonuses, was a six-figure remuneration.

That was more than enough to keep his wife and two daughters in the manner to which they had very quickly become accustomed, and enough to ensure there was plenty left over for him to enjoy himself, doing pretty much whatever he wanted to do.

The markets closed. Brian finalised his daily accounts, noted his profit for the day and turned off his screens.

'Not bad,' he thought, especially as his mind hadn't really been on his job today.

In fact, he had been somewhat distracted all week. He was looking forward to next week when he was attending a 'morale-boosting, team-building event' in the United States. He'd been on them before, knew what to expect and thoroughly enjoyed them.

It was like being back at school, picking on the weaker members of the team, belittling them, mocking them and ensuring that the only team that was built was Team Tottie.

He was still an Alpha male and everyone else on the trading floor had better believe it. Although in case they did, Brian wasted no opportunity to remind them and to reinforce his reputation as the man to respect and follow unreservedly.

"OK, you bunch of faggots, who's turn is it to buy bubbly for the maestro? he shouted to whoever was listening, which was usually everyone.

"Isn't it yours?" said a voice with mock bravado.

"Only if your daily figures are anywhere close to mine," replied Brian instantly. "And we all know that's as likely as you having sex tonight. Well, sex that involves another person, that is," he added after a suitable pause to enable the laughter to build.

And it did. It always did. Brian's jokes were funny. That was an accepted fact. Brian's invitations to go for a drink were really commands. Brian's request for someone to buy was always met.

Not that Brian was mean. He stood his round and was often flamboyantly generous with his bar bill. But he decided when he bought the drinks and it was invariably timed to gain maximum effect - when the bar was full, when entertaining guests, when impressing women or when it reinforced his status as the office silverback.

Brian believed in getting his money's worth out of his money, otherwise, he'd drink someone else's.

The drinking had been relatively mild by normal standards. Brian just wasn't in the mood. His mind was on next week and he still had some last-minute arrangements to make, as well as to do his packing. He left first thing on Saturday morning and he had a family meal planned for tomorrow evening so he needed to get things finished tonight.

He spent the 90-minute drive home on automatic pilot thinking through the following week and how much he was looking forward to the trip. It had been a long time since he'd had a full week to enjoy himself and he was going to make sure he got the most out of every single minute of it.

Chapter 34.

If Rupert Burns thought the first meeting with his lawyer had gone badly, he was completely unprepared for the next meeting, particularly the revelation that his wife had now made a statement to the police.

The couple had not been in contact for weeks, not since she'd sent him a text to say she would contact him when she was able to, and that he should make no attempt to contact her, or it was all over.

Most of what was in the statement was what he'd expected her to say. She knew nothing about the images, she'd never seen them on the computer, she'd taken the computer to be repaired because it was broken, she didn't know what was wrong with the computer, or how it had frozen. She had no knowledge of Rupert taking photos in public places nor had she ever even suspected that he had any paedophilic tendencies.

Although Rupert was initially annoyed that Di had agreed to give a statement at all, particularly without telling him, he was beginning to think that she might have done the right thing and that this was supporting his case. A case that he thought was getting stronger, despite his lawyer's reservations.

This delusion was shattered moments later when his lawyer informed him that his wife's statement also included the revelation that he had taken a number of photographs of her while she was getting changed, and in various stages of undress.

It appeared that the police had found the images of Di on the computer and had asked her about them. She said the photos had been taken at various times over the period of a couple of years. She denied posing for any of them or being complicit in their taking, but she had accepted that she had not complained about the fact he'd taken them because she'd believed they would be kept private and she hadn't wanted to confront him on the subject, which at the time, she'd believed was harmless.

"So, the police now have your own wife saying you have, on a number of occasions, surreptitiously taken photographs of her as she was dressing or undressing," the lawyer was saying. But all Rupert could hear was white noise in his head. This was not good.

Chapter 35.

Lemure opened the door of his apartment. He was sweating heavily, far more than usual, after his morning run. It was humid outside, but he also suspected it might be because he was starting with a cold. This really was the worst possible time for him to fall sick. He didn't need that at this point in his plans. He needed to be fully fit for the weekend.

As he began to towel his head and neck, the phone rang. Lemure let it ring a couple of times and then picked up the receiver.

"Hello," said a voice Lemure didn't recognise. "Is that Nigel Pye?"

"Yes," Nigel replied. "Who is this?"

"Oh hi, my name is Ricky Marriott," replied the voice. "I'm a reporter with the West Lancs Herald, but you might remember me from school. I was a couple of years younger than you but in the same house."

"Er yes, I think so," replied Nigel, hesitantly. "It's a long time ago."

"Yes, time flies doesn't it," continued Ricky, happy that he'd made a connection, however tenuous, and hesitant.

"So how can I help you?" asked Nigel, puzzled as to what had prompted this call from the past.

"Just a brief chat really," replied Ricky. "The thing is I thought I'd pick your brains and see what you think about something."

"Why me?" said Nigel.

"Well, it's a bit bizarre," admitted Ricky. "And to be honest I'm not even sure it adds up to anything anyway. I don't know if you've heard, either on the old boys' grapevine or even on the news, but a couple of the lads in your year have been making the headlines over the past few months."

Nigel had never been tapped into the old boys' network but he was aware of the headlines to which Ricky was referring.

"No, I haven't heard anything," he lied. "What headlines? Which lads?"

"Well," said Ricky. "It started last year when David Stevenson died in a diving accident off a Thai island."

"Oh, actually I did hear something about that," interrupted Nigel. "Very sad," he added with as much sincerity as he could muster.

"Yes, it was," continued Ricky, not detecting the irony in Nigel's reply. "Anyway, since then there's been more bad luck happening to lads in your year, in fact to lads in our boarding house. And, if I remember correctly, they were all actually in your dorm."

"Really? Who?" asked Nigel, interested to hear what the journalist was talking about, and even more interested to hear what he was thinking.

"Well, Terence Nicholson had a heart attack after his business went bust in a poison pie scandal," said Ricky, speaking in the headline way newspaper journalists sometimes adopt without realising they are doing it. "There was also what police think was an arson attack on his factory, which might or might not have been an attempted insurance scam."

Nigel didn't say anything. So Ricky pressed on:

"Now Rupert Burns has been found with a ton of indecent images on his computer, some of them of underage girls, taken in public changing rooms. He was in your dorm wasn't he?"

"Degs? Yes, he was," replied Nigel. "For most of our time there."

"Thought so," said Ricky, "Incidentally why was he called Degs?"

"It was part of the evolution of nicknames," replied Nigel, all too aware of how he'd ended up with the moniker of Porky.

"Burns became Third Degree which got shortened to Degs," explained Nigel, the humour of the derivation had long since worn thin on him.

"Oh, very good," said Steve. "And Poppy was in there too, wasn't he? Higgins, was his name, wasn't it? That's another one I never got."

Nigel sighed. "That's another one on the evolution chain," he explained. "Higgins became Higgy, which sounded like 'Iggy, which morphed into Iggy Pop and then Poppy emerged the other side."

"Funny how you just accept things at school without really questioning them," replied Ricky.

"And ironic, given that's the very place where you should be questioning things," said Nigel, "But if enough people go along with something then so does everyone else. But you didn't ring me to find out how two schoolboys got their nicknames, did you?"

"True." said Ricky, also keen to push on with the purpose of his call. "If I remember correctly, there was you, Tottie, Stevo, Nicho, Degs, Poppy, Gassy and 'Dickie' Davies in your dorm, wasn't there?" said Ricky, reading off a list.

"Well there was for two or three years," answered Nigel. "Gassy started as a day-boy and only became a boarder when his parents divorced and moved abroad, and Dickie wasn't in our dorm for the first couple of years. But yes, those were the ones in our dorm for most of my school years. But, so what?"

"Well, there's more," said Ricky, keen to present as much evidence as he could to justify what even he realised was a flimsy theory. "Remember old Collins, the history teacher everyone hated?"

"Yes" said Nigel cautiously.

"Well, he topped himself after getting caught up in some sort of hate crime scandal. Turns out he'd been posting anti-Islamic material on the internet and making threats against mosques, etc."

"Really?" said Nigel. "I'd never have guessed he held those kinds of views. He wasn't popular, but mainly because he was so strict, and a little vindictive too, but I never detected any extreme racial or religious views."

"No, me neither" admitted Ricky. "It was a bit of a shocker."

"So, what's this got to do with me," asked Nigel.

"Well, nothing really, and I'm not looking for quotes or anything," said Ricky hurriedly.

This was the part of the conversation he had not been looking forward to because it was likely to make him sound an idiot.

"It's just…. well….it just seems a bit of a coincidence that all that bad luck should hit the same group of people within a few months. I mean three deaths and a spectacular fall from grace, happening to three members of the same dorm and a teacher everyone hated."

Ricky trailed off and waited. There was silence.

"Nigel?" said Ricky.

"Yes, I'm here," Nigel replied. "So, what are you thinking?"

"Well, I was wondering if it was perhaps more than a coincidence."

There he'd said it. But he was aware that a more problematic part of the conversation was looming.

"Like what? A conspiracy of some sort?" asked Nigel.

"Maybe," replied Ricky.

"In what way?" Nigel continued. "I don't get it, and I don't see what any of it, coincidence or not, has to do with me, just because I shared a room with them 20 years ago. You're not suggesting we are all cursed or something are you?"

This was crunch time. Ricky either went for it or backed away and the call would have been a waste of time.

"I don't know. Perhaps," he replied. "I mean those three were not exactly popular while we were at school, were they?"

Nigel didn't reply.

Ricky continued: "I mean, Stevo and Nicho were worse but they were all bullies, weren't they?"

Again, Nigel did not respond.

"And, er, well, er, you were a common target for them, weren't you?"

There, it was out and this could end the conversation very quickly.

Nigel did not respond and there was silence for almost 10 seconds before he said: "Everyone got bullied, Ricky. I recall you taking your fair share at times, like the time you were persuaded to put on a face mask and keep it in place by pushing your lips through it, only for Nicho to smack your lips which were protruding through the paper mask. Remember that, Ricky?"

Ricky nodded and then realised Nigel couldn't see him. "Yes, I remember," he muttered.

"It was all prompted because Stevo thought you had big lips, if I recall," continued Nigel. "Hence your nickname - Jagger."

"Yeah, I remember," said Ricky, who had pretty much managed to suppress most of those memories since leaving school, and surprisingly, his lips had never seemed as big once he left school.

"I'm sorry Ricky," said Nigel, "But I'm struggling with this conversation. I don't follow you. These things seem to have happened over the course of more than a year, and in different places, if I'm following you correctly.

"There was a tragic diving accident in Asia, a heart attack somewhere in Yorkshire I assume, a suicide somewhere else and a guy has been caught with kiddy pics in another place. I appreciate the tenuous link but I can't see anything that really connects them.

"And now you're ringing me because three of them used to be in my dorm, and the other taught me - along with thousands of other boys over the years. Are you suggesting there is an actual connection, and more importantly, that the supposed connection involves me?"

Ricky realised how pathetic it all sounded, and regretted getting so carried away with his conspiracy theory that he'd actually voiced it to someone else.

"No of course not," he spluttered. "I was just running it past you to see if you found it odd. I was planning to ring Higgins, Simpson and Davies too, to ask them what they thought. I just managed to find your number first, so you got the first call.

"And you're right, it's stupid. Just desperate for a story, I guess. You know what journalists are like'" he ended lamely.

"Well, I don't know anything about it but from what you've told me it sounds like it's just a weird coincidence to me," said Nigel.

"Yes, you're probably right," said Ricky. "Anyway, sorry to have bothered you, good to catch up. Thanks for talking to me and setting me straight. If you're ever back up here then give me a shout, we can have a pint, or a coffee or something, and catch up properly. I promise I won't talk about any more conspiracy theories."

"I've no plans on being back there," said Nigel, truthfully. "But if I do, I'll look you up," he lied.

"Great, and thanks again," said Ricky hanging up.

Lemure disconnected and reflected on the conversation. Marriott certainly had put two and two together and although he was getting five at the moment, it was an unexpected development.

Lemure did not like anything unexpected. He'd already suffered the unexpected Collins suicide which had shocked him more than he thought.

Fortunately, that had not required any action, nor a change of plan. Lemure hoped enough had been done to put Marriott off the story. He didn't want to have to change his plan to deal with a journalist who didn't have enough news to cover.

Chapter 36.

Shelley Tottingham swung their Lexus 4x4 into the dropping off area at Heathrow airport just before 7.30 on Saturday morning. She'd agreed to drop Brian at the airport rather than insist he get a taxi.

"Making sure I go?" Brian had joked, but there might have been some truth in his comment. Their twin girls were in the back, both wearing headphones and playing on their iPads. They were not very impressed they'd been dragged out of bed at this time on a Saturday morning, 'just to go to the airport'. They'd only stopped complaining when Shelley had promised them a fast-food breakfast on their way home and a sleep-over for their friends that evening.

They barely looked up as Brian got out of the car and took his case from the back. Shelley stayed in the car but at last put down the driver's window signalling she would kiss him goodbye, but that it wasn't going to rival a scene from Love Story.

"Ring me when you get there," she said, more out of habit than genuine concern.

"Of course," he replied. "It will be late tonight though, by the time I land, get to the hotel and sort myself out."

"Whenever," Shelley replied. "Girls say goodbye to daddy."

Brian thought he detected a murmur from the back seat but he couldn't be sure as the car engine was still running so it might have just been that.

"Bye girls," he said. This time there definitely was silence.

Brian had not got to the pavement before the car sped away.

'Good job I didn't walk around in front of it," thought Brian, genuinely unconcerned by the lack of affection his family farewell had elicited. He had no idea what Shelley would do for the week and he wasn't bothered. She had no idea what he'd be doing either, and he smiled as he walked into the terminal.

Terminal 5 was bustling, even at that time. Brian looked at the departures board. His flight was on the second page. A British Airways flight to Atlanta, departing at 1035.

He'd lied to his wife about the departure time to make sure they arrived on time. But she'd been up and about before him, and the burger breakfast promise had prevented too much of a delay from the girls, so Brian was very early. He looked around the concourse and saw a coffee shop where he decided he should kill a little time.

Thirty minutes later, Brian got up, dropped his paper cup in a rubbish bin and left the airport. He walked briskly to the car rental office where he picked up the car he'd ordered on Thursday evening. The car was ordered in his name because he would be required to produce his driving licence. But all other bookings for the coming trip were booked in the name of Aston Haws, a typically Brian in-joke based on the fact his old boarding school house had been called Aston House.

'They may not have been the very best years of his life, but they were damned close,' he thought as he completed the paperwork for the car rental.

And so, at about the same time as Shelley and his beloved offspring were leaving the burger place to drive back home, Brian was driving his hired BMW around the M25 towards the M1. He had a full morning's driving ahead of him but he was energised, liberated, and as excited as a schoolboy to be free for a week.

Lemure felt almost the same way as he signalled and took the left-hand lane to join the M1.

Chapter 37.

Porky was lying in bed, with his head under the covers. It was how he tried to shut himself off from everything that was going on around him. It was a pretty feeble system. A sheet and a blanket were hardly a force-field, nor did they make him invisible - a blanket of invisibility was clearly the stuff of fantasy. Porky's situation was very real and he had to live with it, day after day. Of course, they didn't tease and bully him every day, but the threat was always there. He could never relax. Events could turn in seconds and suddenly he would be back in the spotlight for whatever 'fun' had just been dreamed up for him.

In fact, nothing was happening to him at the moment. They were talking after lights out, something that was forbidden but happened regularly. It usually ended when the dorm prefect arrived to go to bed and so the room fell silent. Finally, everyone could get some peace and properly relax, at least until the morning when tomorrow was always another day. Sometimes it ended with a prefect or master passing the door and hearing the talking. That could end one of two ways - a warning to stop talking and a threat that if anyone was heard again there would be trouble - or a demand to know who was talking because trouble was about to be administered.

Invariably, nobody ever owned up immediately, which might mean the whole dorm being punished, or perhaps the culprits would take their punishment and leave the rest of the room out of it. You could never tell which way it would go, and Porky had suffered more than his fair share of unfair punishments that had nothing to do with him. So, while Porky was happy they were leaving him alone, he remained nervous about their conversation - if you could call Nicho farting and the others trying to guess which teacher would do one that sounded like that, a conversation. The noise was getting progressively louder as more people joined in the laughter, but it meant they were totally caught up in the exercise and so Porky could just lay and think.

But his were unhappy thoughts. It was many months since he'd had any truly happy thoughts, not at school, anyway. He was reflecting on the day, and how many times he'd been the butt of their comments and 'jokes'. Porky had grown used to that. It had been going on since he arrived at the school. What was worrying him now was that the bullying was starting to take on a more physical nature. There'd always been a bit of pushing and shoving and the odd ear flick, or being whipped by a wet towel, which was way more painful than you'd imagine if someone was particularly skilled at it - and Tottie, Stevo and Nicho were all very proficient. If towel flicking ever became an Olympic sport the GB team were all laying within ten yards of Porky at that precise moment. But as they all matured physically, some more quickly and dramatically than others, their behaviour became even more physical. What used to be a dig in the ribs or a clip round the head was now far more likely to be a punch in the stomach or a head lock which caused difficulty in breathing and left the victim with a sore neck. Earlier today Porky had actually been rugby tackled as he walked across the day room, and then two other disproportionately large lumps had fallen on top of him, completely removing all the air from his body. He'd been winded for minutes and still ached from the attack.

The impact of his ordeal at the hands of Tottie and his colleagues had undeniably been having an effect on Porky's mental health for some time, but he was now beginning to fear for his physical health.

Suddenly the door opened. The room fell silent. Porky held his breath. It was the room prefect. The door closed and he walked to his bed without saying anything. They had got away with it for another night.

'So at least that had ended well', thought Porky.

He had no idea how other things would end, or if they would ever end. He knew the 'jokes' would continue. Perhaps they would reduce as they all got older? Perhaps they would intensify and become unbearable?

Porky could really only see things getting worse, and increasingly he worried that someone was going to get seriously hurt as the physical violence increased. Deep down he knew that 'someone' was almost inevitably going to be him. A tear forced its way under the eyelids that he'd closed to shut out the reality of where he was and who was around him. He wiped it away, turned over and tried to take advantage of the only time he ever felt truly secure - when he was asleep.

Chapter 38.

It was nearly 4 pm when Brian checked into the small, family-run hotel on the edge of the Lake District. His journey had taken longer than he'd expected, partly because of heavier-than-usual weekend traffic on the M25, and partly because he'd decided to break his journey with a long, relaxing lunch.

He was in a particularly good mood. His lunch had been excellent, his journey after leaving the M25 had been delay-free, and he had a whole week ahead of him to do the things he liked doing

He didn't unpack completely because he was only staying one or two nights before moving on to new adventures. After what settling in was required, he took a walk around the village, checked out the route of his walk tomorrow and sent a text to confirm his dinner date for that evening.

After a short pause, the reply came back: "Looking forward to it. See ya at 8."

Brian read it and smiled. He'd have preferred 'you' rather than 'ya', but 'hey, he wasn't looking for intellect'. He looked at his watch.

'Time for a leisurely bath, a shave and his phone call home,' he thought as he began walking back towards his hotel.

The phone rang for a while and then went to the answering machine. Brian listened to his own voice explaining how he wasn't able to get to the phone right now but if he left a message, he'd get back to himself.

Brian sighed. He didn't leave a message. Instead, he rang again 5 minutes later. He still had plenty of time before meeting his dinner date and he wanted to actually speak to his wife.

This time the phone rang almost as long, but just before Brian again heard himself, it was answered.

"Hello," said Shelley.

"Hi, it's me," said Brian. "Just checking in. Everything OK?"

"Yes, fine," she replied. "So, you got there OK?"

"Yes, flight was on time and transfer to the hotel was quicker than I expected, so I thought I'd ring now and then grab dinner and an early night," lied Brian.

"Ok," said Shelley, who sounded distracted and disinterested.

"Are the girls OK?" asked Brian, more out of duty than interest.

"Yes, they have some friends here for a sleep-over so they are all upstairs at the moment," said Shelley, hoping Brian knew better than to ask to speak to them as she'd never get them to leave their friends to take a phone call.

"Probably be there all night, apart from trips to the kitchen to stock up on food," she added.

"Yes probably," agreed Brian. "So, what are you up to?"

Brian had no idea why he'd asked that. He didn't really want to know, he didn't care and he had absolutely no doubt that Shelley was more than capable to telling him whatever she wanted him to hear, regardless of how true it was.

"I've got a couple of the girls over so we're just choosing some wine," said Shelley. "Anyway, I'd better go back to them. Have a good time."

Brian hoped they were choosing wine they'd heard of rather than some of his more expensive bottles, but he didn't mention it or Shelley would do an internet search to establish which were the most expensive bottles and target those first.

"OK darling, have fun. And don't forget I probably won't be able to call you for a couple of days. We leave on our camping trek first thing tomorrow and mobiles are banned so I'll call once I'm back in civilisation," he said quickly, before Shelley put down the phone.

"OK fine, see you," she responded, her mind already back in the kitchen with her friends, but at least Brian's threatened interruption to their evening was now over.

"Bye," said Brian, closing the phone with the same thoughts.

Now he could really start to relax and enjoy himself. Just time for another look at the photos of his date and then he'd leave for the restaurant.

Brian, or Mr Haws, as he would be for the entire week, arrived at the restaurant before his date. He was shown to their table and he ordered a whiskey while he waited.

Brian was just savouring his second sip of the warming fluid when he saw the maitre d" speaking to an attractive young blond who had just walked in.   He saw the maitre d" check the reservation book, more for show than because he'd forgotten where he'd seated Mr Haws, nod in the direction of Brian, and begin to show his companion for the evening - and hopefully the night - to the table.

"Sir, your guest has arrived," said the maitre d" unnecessarily.

"Thank you," said Brian and smiled warmly at the blond.

"Hi, Mikey, pleased to meet you," he said, putting out his hand to shake the young man's hand.

"Hi Aston," replied the young man, who was probably only in his early twenties and looked like he regularly worked out.   His voice was alarmingly effeminate, which excited Brian more than he expected. He didn't usually go for that type of man.

As the young man settled his muscular frame into his chair, Brian was reminded of a comment a friend had once made about a similar guy he'd once met at a party - 'Looks like Tarzan, sounds like Jane', and he smiled, both at the memory and at his date.

Mikey wasn't really a blind date. He'd been chosen off the internet and, for once, Brian was relieved that his photo was fairly accurate and recent. Well, it was at least the same man, which was something of a plus and far from guaranteed when splashing around in the murky depths of online dating.

Ok, the voice was a little surprising, particularly given the physique of the guy, but Brian could live with that, and he certainly looked like he'd have plenty of energy. Brian liked that thought even more.

The pair chatted while looking at the menu. Mikey had certainly done his homework. He knew a lot about 'Aston'. Of course, none of it was true, nor any reflection on Brian's 'real life'. But Mikey must have learned every word of Brian's online profile because he knew all his likes and dislikes, interests and hobbies, and other fabrications Brian had included in his profile to make himself sound more attractive to other gay men.

Brian assumed he'd been gay all his life. Certainly, he'd realised at school that he was unusually excited by the sight of other naked boys. He'd fought his tendencies and had not accepted his true sexuality for many years after leaving school.

Nothing sexual had happened while he was at school, although some of his 'play-fighting' had probably strayed over whatever passed for the line between manly horseplay and gay fumbling.

In fact, nothing sexual had happened with another man until shortly before his marriage to Shelley. He'd continued to live the life expected of an alpha male, drinking too much, sleeping with as many women as possible and bragging about both at every opportunity.

In fact, Brian was still living that life as far as everyone who knew him was concerned. He was sure Shelley had no clue, nor his work colleagues, nor any of his friends. He worked very hard to maintain the pretence that he was pure hetero-male, at times having to imagine he was sleeping with a man while having sex with Shelley. That was tricky at first, once he'd admitted to himself that he was gay, but he'd managed it so often that now it was routine.

He wished he could come clean about his secret life, but he thought there was too much at stake and he couldn't risk losing any of it. Not now. Perhaps in a few years when he'd built up enough money that Shelley didn't know about. Then he could leave her, pay the debilitating divorce she'd no doubt demand - and get - and bugger off abroad to live the life he really wanted to live.

But for now, he'd carry on being macho-banker Brian 'Tottie' Tottingham for fifty weeks of the year, and keep escaping when he could to be Aston Haws, the man he really was.

They both ordered the same starter and main course, which Mikey thought was sweet and a good omen for their relationship.

Brian thought it was a little creepy and there would be no relationship after tonight, certainly not after tomorrow night.

Brian had booked two nights at the guest house but had not yet decided whether to move on tomorrow. Mikey's performance tonight would determine the date - not that he knew that.

Brian did not want to pressure his new friend. But he had to admit the boy could talk, unlike many of his online friends who might have the physique of a bodybuilder but were incapable of building a sentence - at least one with a correctly declined verb, appropriate tense and one he was interested in hearing.

But Mikey seemed intelligent and a reasonable conversationalist, if a little too effeminate for Brian's liking. But, he concluded, he really hadn't been chosen to make conversation - that was a bonus which was making the meal more enjoyable.

Their starters arrived - mushrooms in a cheese sauce, or champignons au fromage, as the menu described it.

'How pretentious for a restaurant in the back of beyond' thought Brian, as he looked up from the steaming dish which had been delivered in front of him.

"Ah, mushrooms - the choice of champignons," said Brian. And to his surprise, Mikey laughed. He'd actually got the joke.

"Bon appetite," said Brian, not appreciating the irony of using that expression given his views on pretentious French names on menus.

The couple both started to eat, providing a temporary break in the conversation.

"Are you OK?" asked Brian.

Mikey was as white as a sheet. He had started to sweat and had put down his fork. In the seconds since Brian had noticed the sudden change, Mikey's colour had gone from white to pale green.

"I'm sorry, you'll have to excuse me," he replied, before leaving the table and almost running to the toilet.

'Well,' thought Brian, 'that's a first.'

He continued eating while he waited for his companion to return. Brian finished eating and glanced towards the toilets. Ten minutes had passed. Then fifteen. The waiter asked if everything was alright.

"My companion has had to excuse himself," replied Brian. "Can you take away his starter. Perhaps it could be re-heated on his return?"

"Of course sir, but we will bring a fresh one rather than re-heat this one."

"That's great. Thank you."

Brian again looked towards the toilets but there was no sign of Mikey. He waited another five minutes and then decided he should probably go and check he was ok.

Just as he was getting up and laying his napkin on the table, the maitre d' appeared.

"Sir, I'm sorry but your companion has had to leave," he said. "We sent him home in a taxi. He was most unwell but he didn't want to return to the table, given, err his appearance, err as a result of his illness, sir. He asked me to apologise and to tell you he would contact you later this evening or in the morning."

Brian still involuntarily looked around the restaurant, as if he was the subject of a practical joke, and Mikey was actually hiding somewhere.

The maitre d' seemed to sense Brian's scepticism and added: "Another guest reported that there was someone, err being violently ill if I can phrase it like that sir. When I went to investigate, I found your colleague in something of a state, very embarrassed and anxious to get home and away from such a public place."

"Ok, said Brian. "Thank you for dealing with the matter so discretely, and for letting me know."

"Will sir be leaving too?" asked the maitre d".

"Not before I've finished eating," said Brian, sitting down again. "Can you cancel one of the steaks please - the one medium to well done. Thank you."

Brian didn't take long to process information, nor did he harbour emotions for long either. Perhaps it was his fast-paced occupation. Perhaps he was a selfish git, lacking any real empathy.

Either way, Brian had gone from annoyance to surprise, to disappointment, to annoyed irritation and back to thinking about himself in the short time since he'd got up from the table and then re-seated himself.

'Evening is buggered,' thought Brian, again missing the irony of his thoughts. 'Might as well enjoy the steak, finish the wine and move on to better things tomorrow.'

Chapter 39.

Brian woke at 8 am with a steaming headache and aching limbs. He closed his eyes again but the pounding continued. He reviewed the evening after Mikey had left in such a hurry.

He had still not heard from him, but Brian had almost forgotten the young man. He certainly didn't feel he should contact him to see how he was, given he'd ruined the evening. But he couldn't understand why he felt so rough.

Admittedly he'd finished most of the bottle of wine, and enjoyed a brandy to round off the meal, and he'd had a couple of whiskeys when he got back to his room, while he trawled online to find another 'Mikey' for this evening, but that wasn't enough to cause this degree of a hangover.

He dragged himself out of bed and into the shower. He stayed there for 20 minutes, with his eyes closed. It helped, but only a little.

'Could he be suffering from the same thing that had affected Mikey?' he thought.

'No, he'd be fine,' he concluded, based on little more than machismo. 'It would pass. No need to change his plans.'

Brian was determined to climb a mountain, while he was in the Lakes, well a fell if he was honest, but it would become a mountain if he ever told anyone about the trip. And today was the day when he'd allowed time in his schedule to do it.

He would walk all day, check out tonight and then drive the short distance to Penrith, where he'd reserved a room and arranged another date. But this time there would be no preamble. Brian had simply hired a companion for the night rather than a date.

'Not having another one of the soppy buggers going sick on me,' he thought, as he dressed for his walk.

It was just after 9 am when Brian reversed his hire car out of the hotel car park after checking out. He always chose BMWs when he hired cars because they were reliable and comfortable, despite the rather harder German suspension. Although he felt less than comfortable this morning when he slumped his lethargic body into the driving seat.

He actually jumped slightly as something sharp pricked his bottom - again another phrase that was lost on Brian as he looked at the seat to find the cause of the pain. He couldn't find anything on the leather seat and when he again sat down, he didn't feel anything untoward. Brian dismissed it as his headache was still causing him greater problems.

It was a typical day in the Lake District, which meant it would probably rain soon. But it was a short drive to the foot of the fell Brian had selected for his 'climb', and he was grateful for that. Perhaps once he was out in the bracing open air, he'd feel better and enjoy the day's hike.

He'd spent quite a while researching this walk and he was determined to enjoy it. Apparently, there was a 'hidden lake' near the summit of the fell he'd chosen and Brian loved the idea of any kind of secret.

In reality, nothing remains a secret in the Lake District, where fell walkers have trampled every inch of the landscape, some with little care for its preservation, others with the care and attention it deserved.

So, it wasn't really a hidden lake, just unusual to find it so far up in the fells. But Brian had found a lot of stuff online telling him it was a 'must see'. He'd even had an email from the Cumbria Tourist Board telling him it was the attraction of the month, which rather argued against its hidden status, but that went right over Brian's head, as so much did.

The lake was a key attraction of the Lakes and he was going to see it if it killed him. Perhaps not the best phase given the way he was feeling, but he'd felt worse and survived.

Less than 20 minutes after leaving the hotel, Brian pulled into the isolated car park and gratefully got out of the car. He took a couple of deep breaths and felt a little better. Perhaps it was going to be a good day after all.

He looked at the sky. A few clouds as you'd expect, but none of them was that dark, and anyway, he had waterproofs and basic survival gear in his rucksack.

He put his small rucksack on his back, locked the car, and began the climb which he estimated should take him less than a couple of hours.

Chapter 40.

Lemure slept well and woke refreshed and alert at 6.30 am. He went for a run before sampling the excellent breakfast which consisted of Cumberland sausage, eggs, bacon, black pudding, tomatoes and mushrooms, all washed down with tea that certainly had the strength to get out of the pot, as his grandmother used to say.

He savoured his meal and checked out of his B&B before 8 am. That would give him plenty of time to drive to Brian's hotel before he left for his lake hunt.

Lemure knew it was going to be a good day. It was the day he'd been waiting for, for such a long time. He smiled as he drove and listened to the weather forecast on a local radio station.

It was going to be clear in the morning but the afternoon would bring rain and that would worsen as the day went on, until the evening when conditions on the fells would become more dangerous. There were warnings that the next couple of days would be perfect weather for ducks but walkers were being advised to stay at home.

Lemure smiled again. He prided himself on planning every detail meticulously but even he could not control the weather. That had a mind of its own and listened to no man, so it was encouraging that the climate gods had decreed that the weather should be exactly as Lemure would have wished it to be, on exactly the day he needed it.

It took Lemure less than two minutes to open the door of the blue BMW, insert a needle into the driver's seat, lock the car again and drive away, without seeing a soul or a soul seeing him. He'd checked the area for cameras, but this was rural Cumbria, not a crime-ridden inner city, so that level of security surveillance was an unnecessary expense.

He would soon be out in the open air enjoying the Cumbrian fells, where sheep outnumber people and a man could truly feel alone. Not that that bothered Lemure.

He had lived most of his life alone. It was easier that way, nobody to ask awkward questions. He could do what he wanted, when he wanted, with whom, or without whom, he wanted and take as long, or as short, as he wanted to do it. Lemure appreciated that freedom now that he was alone and it helped him live the life he'd chosen.

He pulled into a fell-side car park and appreciated that there were only a couple of other cars in there. He had his pick of parks but chose to park next to one of the four other cars in the park.

Experience had taught him that people notice cars on their own but nobody paid any attention to a row of cars. Hopefully, a couple more cars would arrive and complete the row before Brian arrived. Lemure got out of the car, locked the door, and began his hike.

Chapter 41.

Porky could hear the sound of sirens in the distance. The two-tones in time with the throbbing in his head. He couldn't see anything and he didn't know where he was. His head was pounding and he could feel something wet on his cheek.

The sirens were getting closer and he could hear voices but he still couldn't see anything. He didn't even know if his eyes were open but he could see bright lights, so bright that he would have shut his eyes if he could, so he assumed his eyes were shut and the lights were somehow on the inside.

The voices were muffled but the sirens were getting louder and then he heard no more, as he again lost consciousness and his head slumped back into the pool of blood that was spreading out across the rough wooden floor.

Porky woke up in the ambulance. He could still hear the sirens but there were no voices. The lights were still there but he could see he was in an ambulance. He could see the blurred figure of a paramedic. She leaned over him and spoke.

"I'm Jane. Can you tell me your name?" she asked, kindly, but with a clinical professionalism that both worried and reassured Porky in equal measures.

He was in no doubt that he was in safe hands but he didn't know why he was in those hands. He couldn't remember anything before he'd heard sirens.

"Nigel," replied Porky, not really knowing where the answer came from.

"Ok Nigel," said the paramedic. "You've had a bang on the head. Can you tell me what happened?"

"No, I don't know," replied Porky. "I can just remember hearing the ambulance. Oh, and some people talking."

"Ok don't worry about it now, just relax and we will be at the hospital soon where they can take a proper look at you."

Porky didn't hear any more. He remained unconscious for the rest of the journey and while he was admitted to A&E.

Chapter 42.

Brian's head was clearing slowly but it was being replaced by dizzy spells and waves of nausea, which were much worse than the headache.

'Perhaps I've got the same food poisoning Mikey had,' he thought as he trudged his way up the fellside. 'Although Mikey's reaction had been instant, and explosive. This was 12 hours later.'

He stopped a few more times than he'd intended, and took numerous drinks from his water bottle, more than he should if it was to last him all day. But once he reached the 'secret lake' he could refill for the descent so he wasn't too worried about running out.

He was still enjoying the macho element of fell walking, man against the elements, despite his nausea. In fact, as long as it didn't get worse, it made it a bigger challenge and would help embellish his account of the trip, although it would be a while before he shared it, given he was meant to be in the States.

Still, he wished he felt a little better so he could enjoy the experience a little more. The rain had held off so far, but the sky was darkening ominously, and he'd felt a few drops of rain in the last ten minutes.

Brian soldiered on as another wave of nausea washed over him. According to his map, he was nearly at the lake. Perhaps a cold drink and a short break would make him feel better. At least well enough to get to the lake and make his descent before the weather turned nasty. He pressed on, oblivious to the fact he was being watched.

After walking for another ten minutes the sky had darkened significantly, and Brian's mood had kept pace with it. He really did feel rough. The nausea was threatening to make its presence felt in a far more physical fashion. He just had to stop.

Brian sat down beside a large rock, which provided some shelter from the wind that had begun to gather force. He reached for his water bottle and removed the top. It was empty.

"Shit," he said, even though there was nobody within earshot.

"Shit, shit, shit," he exploded, and his expletives echoed around the fells. Brian threw his water bottle and slumped back against the cold slate, closing his eyes.

"Got a problem mate?" said a voice.

Brian opened his eyes with a start. His vision was blurred but he could see a man standing in front of him. The man was dressed in full wet weather gear with a buff concealing much of his lower face.

"Sorry didn't mean to startle you," said the man, who could see Brian was more than startled. "Can I help?" he continued.

"Err sorry about that," replied Brian, a little embarrassed by his childish outburst. "I've run out of water and, to be honest, I don't feel too good."

Oh dear. Here have some of mine," said the stranger, reaching for a water bottle in his pack. "Are you going to be OK to get down or would you like me to help you," he asked.

Brian tried to pull himself together. He'd take the water but there was no way he was going to allow himself to be escorted off the mountain. That wasn't the end of the day he'd seen for himself in any scenario.

"Thanks, I'll take a drink if I can," said Brian, taking the proffered bottle. "But I'm sure after a few minutes sitting here, I'll be good to go."

"Are you sure," asked the man. "You look very pale. I am on my way down now so can easily walk with you. The weather is turning. This afternoon looks like being a nasty one," he added looking at the sky as if checking his forecast.

Brian drank heavily from the bottle and it did seem to help.

"Yes, I'm sure," he replied. "I'm keen to see the hidden lake before I head down and I'm feeling a little better. Probably just a little dehydrated."

"Well at least let me give you some of my water in case you need more before you get to the lake, which is only about five minutes over that next ridge." said the man, walking to retrieve the water bottle Brian had thrown in his frustration.

The man refilled Brian's bottle from one of his own and after again checking Brian felt well enough to be left on his own, he made his way down the fell side.

"Thank you," said Brian. "I appreciate your kindness and help," he added, genuinely appreciative of the man's kindness. Giving and receiving kindness were not usually things which featured largely in Brian's life, but this water was a real lifesaver.

Lemure lowered the binoculars and sighed. The master strategist, the meticulous planner, the man who never let anything, or anyone, derail his mission, had nearly been scuppered by a good Samaritan.

'What were the chances on a mid-week day, with poor weather, that someone would stumble upon Brian in his present condition' he asked himself. 'And offer to help him too.'

'Thank God, he's an arrogant prick and has no idea how bad conditions can get on these fells, especially if the clouds cut visibility to a few feet,' he thought, as he stood up from his vantage point and began making his way towards the lake.

Chapter 43.

Porky regained consciousness on a ward. The bright lights in his head had dimmed and the pounding had subsided to 'just' a terrible headache.

He could remember falling to the floor with a pain above his right eye but he couldn't remember what had caused it. He was in the day room.

'That's right,' he recalled. 'He was in the day room. Had he fallen? Had he tripped and hit his head? No, he could remember the pain before he hit the floor.'

Porky looked around the private room and took in all the machines and medical equipment which surrounded him. He closed his eyes and the pain in his head eased.

Then he heard Tottingham's voice.

"Tell them you fell, Porky, he said. "Remember you fell."

Porky quickly opened his eyes but there was no-one there. He looked round the room but he was alone. But he could still hear Tottingham.

The words echoed around his head. "Tell them you fell, Porky. Remember you fell."

Porky realised he was getting flashbacks and the words were not being said now, they were a memory.

And with that realisation came a torrent of memories as if a blockage had been removed. They came flooding back into his mind, arriving in reverse as his memory rebuilt itself.

He remembered what had happened. He'd been reading in the day room. Tottingham had walked in, closely followed by

Nicholson and Stevenson. They must have been playing cricket because Tottingham was carrying a cricket bat and Nicholson was bouncing a tennis ball.

Even as he relived the memories, Porky felt the usual dread he suffered when he saw them. They saw him and he knew the dread would be realised. They headed straight for him.

"Hey Porky, fancy playing cricket?" said Nicho.

"No thanks." replied Porky, with no expectation that the answer would be heeded.

"Oh, go on, you'll love it," said Tottie. "Come on, get up, you can be the wickets."

Nicho exploded with laughter, which grew louder as Tottie prodded Porky with the cricket bat.

"Come on, up you get," added Stevo, as Tottie's prods became hits.

Porky stood and began to walk towards the door. Nicho blocked his way.

"You're not going anywhere" he said. "You're going to play cricket with us" and he threw the tennis ball at Porky from two yards away. It hit his head and bounced behind some lockers.

"Now look what you've done," said Tottie. "You've lost our ball. You'll have to be the ball now." And with that Tottie swung the bat and hit Porky across the thighs.

Porky continued to try to get out of the room, as he knew this was only going to get worse and wouldn't stop unless someone else came into the room.

But as he tried to get to the door Nicho pushed him back into the centre of the room. Porky stumbled and nearly fell. That stumble coincided with Tottie again swinging the bat. The bat *struck Porky just above the eye and he went down like a sack of potatoes.*

He could hear talking but all he could make out were the words: "Tell them you fell, Porky. Remember you fell." And then everything went black and silent.

Chapter 44.

Brian could see the lake now. His joy at seeing it was completely swamped by his relief, and if he was honest, a tinge of disappointment that it really wasn't that big. The photos must have been taken by an estate agent because they managed to make it look much bigger than it really was. He stopped at the brow of a hill and looked down at the water in the hollow beneath him. He took a deep breath and immediately felt faint, swayed a little, before regaining his balance. A wave of nausea washed over him and he was violently sick.

Brian slumped to the ground while the fells revolved around him. He had never felt like this before. This must be connected to the horrors that had befallen his prospective lover last night.

Brian wished he'd had a little more sympathy for Mikey, and as he wallowed in his own sickness, he wondered for the first time how the young man was today. Empathy was an alien concept for Brian.

Perhaps he was just trying to work out how long he was going to be affected by the bug, or parasite, or whatever had infected his system. But in a rare moment of compassion, Brian resolved to message Mikey as soon as he got back to the car to check how he was.

He reached for his water bottle and was surprised to find it was already empty.

'Not again,' he thought as he looked down at the lake, and then at his watch. It had taken Brian more than three hours to get to the lake, much longer than he'd expected. But then he hadn't thought he'd be this sick so perhaps he hadn't done too badly. He consoled himself with that thought that it would be much quicker on the way down.

Brian looked at the sky. It was much darker now, the wind had really picked up and it didn't look too good at all. He looked around him in the hope of seeing some blue sky. Nothing.

The picture was the same wherever he looked, and from where he was sitting, he could see for miles. Well, he would have been able to see for miles, if the visibility was good enough. In fact, it was getting pretty murky.

Brian exhaled heavily and got to his feet, as he made an instant decision. He would go to the lake, refill his water bottle, and then go straight down the mountain, even if he didn't end up at the car park where he started. He could always get himself back to his car.

The important thing now was to get off the mountain. But first he had to get water. He was drinking so much he'd never make it down without another drink. He swayed a little as his vision blurred and the fells once again did a pirouette around his head.

He set out unsteadily down to the lake. As usual, when walking in the fells, distance was deceiving, so it took Brian ten minutes to get to the edge of the water.

He was now sweating heavily, despite the dropping temperature. His vision was no longer just blurred. He was now seeing double. Brian collapsed by the edge of the lake and crawled the rest of the way towards the water.

The lake was lapping against the hillside. One side had a pebbled shoreline, the other a drop down into the water. Brian's approach had brought him in on the opposite side to the shore, but the water was only about a foot below the edge of the rock so he could easily reach down and fill his water bottle.

He did this three times, drinking the ice-cold water as if his life depended on it. Once he'd finished the third container, he again reached down to fill it for his return journey.

It was as he was leaning over the edge of the lake and reaching down into the water for the fourth time, that he felt something around his neck. He saw it flash in front of his eyes without realising what it was. But now it was tightening around his neck.

Brian dropped the bottle and both hands instinctively grabbed at his neck. He felt a rope but it was tight around his neck, too tight for him to get his hands between the rope and his skin.

Brian managed to roll over onto his back, just as he heard a large splash behind him. The rope became even tighter and began cutting into his neck.

"Thought you wouldn't want to come all this way and not have a swim Tottie," said a voice.

Through his double vision, Brian could just make out a man leaning over him.

'Was it the guy who'd helped him earlier?' Brian hoped, while at the same time his brain was screaming that was illogical.

"After all, we all know how much you love swimming," said Lemure, as he picked up Brian's feet. "Hope the temperature is to your liking," he added. "Oh, and don't worry. If anyone asks, I'll remember to tell them you fell."

And with that, Brian felt himself being tipped into the icy lake. Just before his head hit the water, he heard his mobile bleep with an incoming text. Then he plunged into the water as the rock attached to his neck took him down to the bottom.

The icy water caught what was left of his breath after the rope had restricted his intake, and with the sickness draining his energy reserves, Brian simply didn't have the strength or resolve to survive.

Chapter 45.

Mikey put his phone back on the kitchen table. He was still upset that Aston hadn't called or messaged him to find out how he was after his traumatising and embarrassing exit last night.

His first thought had been to ignore it and move on but Mikey was nothing if not courteous and a man of his word. He'd told the maitre d" to tell Aston that he'd message him to tell him how he was.

So, bastard though he was, that's exactly what he'd just done, although he'd failed to keep the edge out of the tone of the text.

'Thought u might like to know I'm still alive. Thanks for not asking. Clearly your mind was only on one thing - U!!! Hope u didn't get what I got.'

OK, it was a little childish but Mikey felt better after sending it. And actually, he was better than just still alive. He felt much better this morning. He'd been really rough all night and had been sick until his stomach was empty. But after a shower, scrubbing his teeth to remove the taste of bile, and three cups of tea, he was beginning to recover.

Mikey looked around his kitchen. It was a mess. Well, a mess by Mikey's fastidious cleanliness standards. In fact, there were a couple of cups to be washed, his jacket and shoes from last night where he'd left them before taking up camp in the bathroom.

There was also the bottle of pills which Mikey usually took before a date. He'd taken two last night but had been surprised to find they were the last two in the bottle. He was sure he had about a dozen or so the last time he looked. In fact, he was still sure. He picked up the bottle and looked again even though it was obvious as soon as he picked it up that it was empty.

Mikey shook his head.

"I'm losing it," he said out loud. "Too much partying, and I'm going doolally."

Mikey really had been sure he had more tablets in that bottle. Just as he'd been sure he'd locked the back door yesterday afternoon when he went to the get his hair cut. But when he got back it had been unlocked.

"Weird," he said, as he began dialling his supplier to order some more tablets.

Chapter 46.

The sky was pitch black and the rain was torrential by the time Lemure got back to the car park. It had turned into what most people would regard as a horrible day, but to Lemure it was close to perfect. He felt like a weight had been lifted from his shoulders. He barely noticed the conditions, other than to reflect that nobody would be venturing on to the fells until tomorrow at the earliest.

There were only two cars left in the car park - two BMWs. One he'd driven there this morning and the other was the one Brian had hired, and would not be returning.

Lemure walked to his car, opened the boot and dropped his backpack inside. He then closed it and walked to the hire car.

It took Lemure seconds to open the car, using a gadget which could be configured to open any car operated by a remote. The device had detected the correct settings this morning, so now it was already a preset and it opened the car on the first press of the button.

Lemure walked to the driver's side, opened the door and reached under the driver's seat to remove the syringe he'd placed there this morning. He looked at the syringe and noted that the needle was not broken, and it was empty. No wonder Brian had been so groggy on his way up the fell.

Lemure couldn't be sure how much liquid would be injected when Brian had sat on the needle so he'd filled it with more than he needed just to be sure. Clearly, Brian's weight had been more than enough to depress the plunger fully, injecting all the syringe's toxic contents into his backside.

Grudgingly, Lemure was quite impressed by how Brian had managed to struggle on so far. That was a lesson for him. If the toxin had stopped Brian continuing to the lake, or he'd been less determined, Lemure would not have been able to get his body into the lake. It also explained why it had been so easy to sneak up on Brian. He must have already been feeling like death warmed up.

'Well, he wouldn't be feeling like death warmed up anymore' reflected Lemure, reaching inside his jacket for a plastic bag, as he sat inside the car to keep out of the rain.

He was still wearing gloves but they were soaked so he did not want to open the bag and take out the paper that it contained because it would get wet. Instead, he opened the bag and shook the paper onto the passenger seat.

Then, he carefully wiped everything he'd touched with a duster he found in the car and got back out into the rain. He quickly dried the driver's seat, which had got wet from his waterproofs, before locking the car and walking back to his car, smiling.

He still had some things to do but they could wait until he'd got back to his hotel and had had a nice hot bath. Lemure chuckled at the irony of the thought.

He started the car and pulled out of the car park, leaving Brian's BMW alone amongst the growing puddles.

Chapter 47.

Porky knew that 'getting to the bottom of things' rarely did that. It usually barely scratched the surface until enough corroborating facts were established to point towards a conclusion which was acceptable.

So, when the inquiry into his 'accident' was launched he knew it would establish a truth that was far from it. Assuming it was an accident at the start of the investigations was a significant pointer towards the conclusion that was the most desirable to the school establishment.

When he was finally asked what he could remember about the incident, it was only after he'd been told what Tottie, Stevo and Nicho had already said. So already there were three people, all with clear recollections and no recent history of a head injury, all telling the same story about events in the day room.

On the other hand, there was someone who was still recovering from a serious blow to the head, who had been drifting in and out of consciousness while he was taken to hospital, and who had no memory of what happened in the hours after the event.

Porky was not stupid. He knew the deck was already stacked against him so he played the hand that he'd been forced to accept. He made no mention of the reckless and brutal swing of the cricket bat at his head, said nothing about the lead up to that blow, or all the other incidents that had plagued his school life.

He told them what they wanted to hear, and what they were already convinced had happened, because the 'facts' they had already established all pointed that way anyway.

Porky had been leaving the day room and tripped. He fell and hit his head on a desk as he fell. That was the version of events that was already the accepted one. It just needed Porky's endorsement. So, he gave it.

Nobody challenged that version of events because there was nobody else present who could challenge it, even though there wasn't anyone who really believed it.

But it was a school, not a murder scene, and so nobody checked the desk or the bat for forensic evidence. There was no camera to dispel the lie that was being accepted as the truth.

But, as Porky knew all too well, when enough evidence pointed in a certain direction then few people were keen to delve any deeper, certainly not to get to the bottom of things. This was a lesson he'd learned the hard way, repeatedly. If everything pointed in a certain direction then most people were more than happy to look the same way, without questioning the logic.

Chapter 48.

Lemure had spent more than an hour in the hotel bath. He'd topped it up a number of times, so the longer he'd been in there, the hotter it had seemed to get. For the first 20 minutes, he'd just lay there, warming up. Then he'd started reflecting on his mission while enjoying a couple of glasses of wine.

He was pretty pleased with himself so far. The mission could still go wrong, of course, and there were lots more things in play which could change the outcome but so far it had gone smoothly.

Through constant monitoring of Brian's email and online accounts, Lemure had easily identified Mikey, an aspiring writer who was really just trying to pluck up the courage to leave the county of his birth and head for a big city. He was conflicted because undoubtedly a big city, or even a decent sized town, would enable him to be himself and perhaps find a loving partner, rather than having to make do with visiting lovers. But he was still caught up in the romantic notion that true writing could only be done in wild, unforgiving surroundings. Too much Wordsworth and Bronte at school, Lemure suspected.

Breaking into Mikey's home had been almost too easy. No complicated locks, alarms or cameras in this part of rural Cumbria.

How Lemure wished we could return to that time when everyone left their doors unlocked. He wasn't sure it had ever really been like that, certainly not in cities, but in the countryside, the focus on security still left a lot to be desired, which as far as Lemure was concerned, made his life a whole lot easier.

By monitoring Mikey's online presence - public and private - he'd found out about his occasional drug use, usually before dates. It had therefore been a simple matter of emptying the bottle of his remaining stimulants and replacing them with two powerful emetic drugs, designed to induce vomiting.

They were more powerful than Ipecac syrup, which used to be readily available over the counter, but because of their primary function, all traces of them were removed quickly, along with everything else in the stomach. Not that there would ever be any checks done. It just looked like a bad bout of food poisoning, and Mikey would be almost back to normal by now.

But the drugs had worked a treat. They had removed Mikey from the scene and stopped him becoming a complication. Lemure could not predict whether Mikey would have stayed the night with Brian, or just a few hours. He didn't want Brian's schedule today to be affected by Mikey's presence, so he'd ensured it hadn't.

Lemure realised he'd been in the bath for more than an hour, he'd either have to top it up with hot water again or get out. His wine glass was empty and although there was half a bottle left, the evening was still young so he didn't want to polish off the bottle this early.

Reluctantly he got out of the bath, dried himself and slipped on the hotel towelling robe. He put on the kettle and sat on the bed.

His mind again became reviewing his mission. It had been almost a year since he'd started his work. All prompted by the bizarre underwater death of David Stevenson, off the coast of Thailand.

Not that Lemure had had anything to do with that death. That was a tragic accident, but then weren't they all. But it had been the catalyst which had put Lemure on a quest for vengeance.

He'd been amazed at the strange circumstances of Stevenson's death but even more intrigued by the relative lack of investigation into something as serious as a death, if the circumstances all seemed to point in the same direction.

If you could get the circumstantial evidence to point at a cause, then most investigators were too idle, or lacked the motivation, to challenge the seemingly obvious.

That realisation had prompted Lemure to consider the chances of anyone seriously challenging a series of apparently unconnected random accidents and misfortunes which could befall a group of people. And if ever there was a group of people who deserved a series of random accidents and misfortunes to befall them, it was Tottie's band of malicious acolytes.

First, Lemure had to find the group which had dispersed like bacteria into the community after leaving school. This had proved relatively quick and easy as most of them hadn't strayed far from their places of birth. He'd found a wealth of information about their lives, occupations, relationships and other data which had become common currency thanks to social media.

Once they were all located, and basic facts and figures about their lives duly researched, Lemure set about compiling a more detailed dossier on each one. This involved electronic surveillance, bugging their homes and offices, hijacking their online communications, including the exchanges that went via hidden servers designed to make them more protected than your average hotmail account.

He had probed every aspect of their existences until he believed he knew all there was to know about them. He certainly knew enough to identify their weaknesses. And that was what had helped to push Nicholson to the top of the list, that and Lemure's belief that he'd be the easiest.

But this ambitious vendetta had been new to Lemure back then. He was already an accomplished hacker, talented investigator and had most of the right personal attributes; patience, cool head, determination, vindictiveness and the ability to lie and deceive.

He also understood how people thought, and reacted. He could read people like a book. But he had no real experience of actually doing any of this stuff 'in the field', as it were.

So, Lemure practised, and practised, and practised some more. Barely a day passed when he didn't adopt a new personality, work on a different accent, develop another scam or put himself to the test using real people. It was like living in a computer game, except it was real.

The practice missions had taught him a lot. Planning was never a waste of time. You couldn't have too much information about someone. Always to be alert to the unexpected and to have a number of fall-back options which could be used instantly if you ran into problems.

But despite all the lessons he'd learned, Lemure now accepted he'd overcomplicated his assault on Terence Nicholson. The poisoning scandal, on top of his massive financial problems, would have been enough. The company would have gone bust. It was going that way without Lemure's help.

Nicholson would have self-destructed, and either had a heart attack naturally, or Lemure could have helped one along without drawing any undue attention. All the 'evidence' seemingly pointed in the same direction, which was all he needed. The arson was an unnecessary risk, and one he would not take again.

It had also taken longer than he'd wanted, given he had to get a job in the factory. That was harder than he'd expected too. It was while he was working his way into that role, that Lemure had broadened the mission.

It was then that he decided that if it was payback time for Tottie et al, then it made sense for him to clear up all his grudges. This had brought his ex-wife Diane, and his old history teacher into the frame.

His ex was a no-brainer. He'd never forgiven her for cheating on him, and the pain was made all the more acute by the pillock she'd married. He would never forgive her, nor could he ever forget not only what she'd done but the way she'd done it, leaving without much of a fight, without really trying to put things right, whatever that might have involved.

Of course, he wouldn't have accepted her efforts, or her apology, because he'd acted swiftly to throw her out, but even a token gesture would have been nice. And to pile on the embarrassment, she'd chosen someone he'd been at school with to be her knight in shining armour.

As far as Lemure was concerned, if Rupert Burns was the answer, then it must have been a bloody stupid question. But, however much it still festered, he couldn't actually bring himself to hurt her, well not physically anyway.

Targeting Burns was easier, much easier, given what a prat he was, what a prat he'd always been, and it might also do her a favour. Not that Lemure particularly wanted to do her a favour, nor did he want her back. But it would be good to make it obvious to everyone, including her, what a mistake she'd made in hitching herself to Burns.

That part of his mission was still incomplete but that was only because justice moved at a slower pace than most people would prefer. It was all still on track, and that's all that mattered. The damage was mainly done however the rest of the events played out.

Burns had been arrested and charged with possessing indecent images. Di was still living with her mother but, according to her emails, was actively looking to rent a small flat, rather than move back into the marital home.

She'd told the police about Burns sneaking photos of her undressing, which while not particularly significant in itself as far as the charges went, effectively killed any hope Burns might have had that she would help his case.

He was still waiting to see if the police added any further charges but, as far as Lemure was concerned, the damage was done.

Burns was ruined, branded a sex offender, and there wasn't a snowball in hell's chance of him living happily ever after with Lemure's ex.

Job almost done but Lemure didn't like loose ends so he couldn't quite close the file on Rupert Burns just yet, although there may not be much more, he had to do to see the story to a successful conclusion. He only had to watch the end game play out as he was sure it would.

James Collins, on the other hand, was not Lemure's finest hour. He still had flashbacks and thoughts about how he could have handled it differently. Once or twice he'd even questioned whether he was right to include Collins on the list at all, but those doubts were quickly dismissed. Collins had been a vindictive bully who abused his position of trust to humiliate and be-little hundreds, if not thousands, of impressionable boys over the years. He deserved his payback.

He perhaps did not deserve to end his days quite so early. But that had been his decision, not one Lemure had mapped out for him. Some things just could not be predicted or controlled.

Fate, you could call it. Destiny. Whatever it was, Lemure was still struggling to forget it, but he was starting to cope better with it. He was sure that in time, it wouldn't gnaw at him quite so much. He certainly wasn't going to let it tarnish today's accomplishment.

'Today had certainly gone much better,' thought Lemure, as he got up to dress for dinner, but not before he enjoyed another glass of that Malbec.

Chapter 49.

Rachel and Emma Tottingham were arguing about everything, and nothing, like 10-year-old twins are prone to do whenever they are together. They had been bickering almost non stop all weekend so Shelley had been delighted when they'd left for school on Monday morning.

But the war of words had continued on Monday evening, again on Tuesday, and here they were on Wednesday evening, verbally tearing chunks out of each other again, over some trivial difference between them.

Shelley was in the kitchen, enjoying her second glass of wine. She hoped a combination of the wine and the distance between the twins and her would muffle most of the incessant whining. It wasn't working too well.

"Shut up, you skanky bitch," echoed through to the kitchen, prompting Shelley to decide enough was enough. She stormed into the playroom, taking the girls by surprise.

"Right," she shouted. "That's enough of that kind of language. We will have no more 'bitches' in this house."

"Great, when is she leaving?" replied Rachel, quick as a flash. Rachel had been the one who'd uttered 'the word too far'.

Shelley was surprised, partly at what a great response it was, especially from a 10-year-old, and partly because it reminded her of a line from the Oscar-winning film Three Billboards Outside Ebbing Missouri.

Ok, the word used in the film was one letter further through the alphabet and of a much higher calibre expletive than 'bitch'. But nevertheless, it was close.

'Could she have seen the film on DVD or somewhere?' thought Shelley, but she dismissed the question instantly as an irrelevant aside, and instead concluded Rachel was going to be an even bigger handful as she grew older, too sharp for most would-be boyfriends. Shelley stifled a smile.

'But not sharp enough to know she should practise her witty put-downs on someone other than her mother,' she thought.

"You are the only one of us who seems to want to earn that description so I suspect suggesting anyone moves out won't work out too well for you," said Shelley.

"So, Emma you can stay here. Rachel, you go to your room. You can be together again in a couple of hours when we have dinner, but not before. And by then I want all your homework finished," she added.

"Oh, that's so unfair," said Rachel. "You always take her side."

"She wasn't the one who thought it was clever to speak like an extra from a rap video," replied Shelley. "That's why you're going to your room. And if you think it's worth discussing any further then that's where you'll be every night this week as soon as you come home from school. Your choice."

Rachel stomped her way to the door muttering something which sounded suspiciously like 'I hate you'.

As she got to the door, she turned and said: "When's my dad back anyway?"

"Not for a few days," said Shelley, "But he's not going to help you. He wouldn't want to hear you speaking like that, so go to your room and I'll call you when it's time for dinner."

Rachel seemed to consider slamming the door but instead shut it a little hard but not enough to bring more punishment.

"And don't think you've got away with everything," said Shelley, turning towards Emma.

"You were both behaving like spoiled brats, she was just the one who took it too far. So, get on with your homework."

Shelley returned to the sanctuary of the kitchen and the restorative effects of her Sauvignon Blanc. But as she took a comforting drink, and sighed at the new sense of calm that had descended on the house, she thought of Brian.

It was probably the first time she'd even considered him since she'd spoken to him on Saturday evening. He'd said he would call when he was back in civilisation, as he called it. She rarely paid much attention to what he said but she was sure the camping element of the trip had only been for a couple of days. Surely, he was back in mobile range by now. 'Why hadn't he called?'

Shelley was surprised to find how concerned she was about his lack of contact. If he had called, she'd have barely listened to anything he said, but the fact he hadn't called, irritated her.

She wasn't worried. After all, if anything had happened to him, they would have contacted her. No, this was just Brian being a selfish git.

She finished her glass of wine and decided if he didn't ring tonight, she would ring him tomorrow, if only to claim the moral high ground that she'd had to ring him because he had been so selfish as not to call her and the girls.

She even considered calling now in case he did call and remove some of her moral outrage, but the thought of another glass of white took priority and she let her main income source slip out of her mind again.

Chapter 50.

Lemure was back in his immaculate and fashionably decorated apartment. He casually browsed photos on his computer as he waited for the kettle to boil, but they no longer held the attraction for him that they once had.

It was 10 years since his wife had disappeared from his life, but he had to admit he had always got a thrill from looking at the almost pornographic photos of her which he still had.

Perhaps it was the fact that he'd had her best years and the photos were a testimony to that. Whoever she was with in the future would never see her as he'd seen her, nor could they even see her like that because he had the only record of how she looked all those years ago. The fact that she'd also had his best years never entered Lemure's self-obsessed brain.

Perhaps it was because she didn't know he had them. Or maybe she did. Maybe she would quite like the idea that he still found her sexually attractive.

Lemure would never know because she would never know he had them. For a while, after too many consoling drown-your-sorrows drinks, he'd considered using them as revenge porn, but it seemed such a cheap shot.

He'd also not worked out a way of using them without them being traced back to him. She would recognise the pictures, remember the drunken evenings when they'd taken them, and know there was only one person in the world who had access to them. Or so he assumed.

Once he'd sobered up, he realised the wisdom of the old saying 'keep your powder dry', and it was empowering to have something he could use if he ever needed it, or if spite ever suppressed his other more logical emotions.

As events had developed, he'd found an opportunity to use one of the photos, heavily photoshopping out the background and cropping out her head, to plant the seed of suspicion in Burns' head, via his photo stash.

The photo had also been a useful way to introduce the virus which crashed his computer, because Lemure reasoned Burns would not be able to avoid opening the photo. And once opened, the file it contained downloaded all those additional incriminating photos onto his hard drive, before launching the virus.

He switched out of the photo album and checked the online news, not the national and international news which he checked routinely every morning, but the local news in his area of interest.

He had been waiting for an update on the story which had gone quiet for a few weeks. He wasn't too bothered. He knew how it would end but it would be good to get closure on it. Lemure hated loose ends and Rupert Burns was certainly a loose end.

So, he was particularly pleased to see an article on the inept specimen and one which was to his liking.

Lemure read with interest that Rupert Burns had appeared in court. It seemed he had agreed to plead guilty to the possession of offensive photos.

Lemure read the report of the facts as outlined in court, most of which he knew because he'd been intimately involved in creating them. Burns had received a one-year prison sentence, suspended for two years, largely because his lawyer had managed to persuade the court that his client was a changed man and was not a risk to the public.

Lemure was impressed. That must have been a hell of a performance, particularly in the current climate of public outrage against anything remotely linked to paedophilia.

Reading between the lines of the report, Lemure assumed the police had been unable to prove the photos had been taken in any specific location, or that Burns had taken them.

Nevertheless, his lawyer couldn't stop Burns being put on the sex offenders register and that was sufficient for the council to dismiss him. To Lemure, that was a job well done.

Lemure would doubtless have felt an even warmer glow of satisfaction had he known that Rupert had also been sentenced to a life of ostracism in his community. He would never become the pillar of the community he aspired to be, and his wife had filed for divorce. Di's lifeboat had finally sunk.

Chapter 51.

Shelley dialled Brian's mobile for the third time in 30 minutes. Nothing. No answer. No dial-tone. No nothing.

'Strange' she thought. 'There's usually a voicemail or something. If he'd turned it off it would surely go to voicemail.'

She had no idea where he was staying. Atlanta somewhere, but that wasn't much use. There would be dozens of hotels and they'd all be full of conferences and groups of workers enjoying corporate rates. She almost wished she'd paid more attention to the details of his trip. Too late now.

Shelley didn't really know many people at Brian's firm, in fact, she'd made a point of avoiding them whenever possible. She had the number for his PA. Well, she wasn't Brian's PA, the team shared her. Shelley wondered how literally the team had taken that job description.

She didn't envy Ellie working with that group of Neanderthals. She shuddered at the thought of being at their beck and call all day, as she dialled Ellie's direct line.

It must seem like a week off for the poor girl when they were all off on their team building jolly. 'Unless she'd had to go with them, she thought as the phone rang.

"Hello, investment team, Ellie speaking," said the voice at the other end of the line. Clearly, she'd been left out of the team building, which Shelley was sure would suit Ellie just fine.

Shelley had spoken to Ellie a couple of times when she'd had to leave a message for Brian but they really didn't know each other.

"Hi Ellie, it's Shelley Tottingham, Brian's wife," she said. Much as she enjoyed all the things that came with being married to Brian, she hated being defined by him, but she figured this was one time when admitting she was married to him would speed up the conversation and guarantee more attention.

"Oh, hi Shelley," said Ellie, "How are you? It's ages since I've seen you. That summer party last year, wasn't it?"

Shelley had no idea, and couldn't even remember meeting Ellie. But now wasn't the time to play catch up. She'd worked herself into the right frame of righteous indignation overnight and she wasn't about to lose that in a cosy chat about a barbecue she only vaguely remembered.

"Yes, it probably was," she replied. "Sorry to bother you but I'm trying to reach Brian. His mobile doesn't seem to be working. Do you have another number for him please?"

She felt a little silly having to ask for contact numbers for her husband. Surely a good wife would know where he was. She dismissed the thought. A good husband would have called. A good husband would have made sure she knew how to contact him in an emergency. A good husband didn't just go AWOL. They would be among the many points she made when she finally managed to speak to him.

"Sorry he's off this week," replied Ellie, a little hesitantly.

"Yes, I know that," said Shelley, a touch of irritation creeping into her voice. "But do you have a number for the hotel where they're staying?"

"Er, no sorry," said Ellie, clearly confused by something. "I just know he's off this week. I don't know which hotel he's in… or even where he's gone, for that matter."

Shelley sighed audibly.

"Well do you have the mobile number of anyone else who's on the trip?" she asked, clearly becoming more irritated.

Unfortunately, Shelley's growing irritation was not helping Ellie's confusion, which seemed to be growing at a similar pace.

"Er trip?" she said. "Sorry, what trip? I don't know anything about a trip."

"The team building trip to the States," snapped Shelley. "How many bloody trips have you got on the go. I thought it was a financial company, not a bloody holiday company."

"I'm really sorry Shelley," said Ellie, whose confusion was off the scale by now. "I don't know anything about a team-building trip to the States, or anywhere else. I just know he's off this week.

"I can put you through to one of Brian's team. He might have told them where he was planning to go on holiday."

"Wait a minute," said Shelley, her irritation beginning to turn itself into almost as much confusion as Ellie was experiencing.

"Isn't his team with him?"

"No. They are all here. Except for Brian who's on holiday," mumbled Ellie, beginning to realise what she'd just done.

She was going to be in a pile of trouble when Brian got back. He'd clearly disappeared for a week without telling his wife.

'Well serves him right' thought Ellie, regaining some assurance.

"As I said, I can see if any of them know where he was going but if you don't know then I doubt he's told anyone here."

Shelley felt like she was going to be sick, and Ellie's little barb hadn't helped. She felt stupid, humiliated, and wished she'd never made the call.

'Cheating bastard' she thought. 'There was no other explanation'. But the last thing she wanted was Ellie asking around and making it clear to everyone what had happened.

"No, it's OK," said Shelley, recovering her wits as quickly as she felt her anger rising.

"I think I've stumbled into a surprise he's been planning," she lied. "Don't mention it to anyone. I don't want to spoil the surprise so I'll just wait for him to call. Sorry to have bothered you. Thanks".

Shelley ended the call as quickly as she could and put down the phone.

She might have stopped Ellie dishing the juicy bit of gossip around the team, or perhaps she'd just made it a little spicier. Her first reaction was embarrassment, with anger quickly replacing it, followed by thoughts of revenge.

'So, if this is how he wants to play it,' she thought 'Let's up the ante and give him some explaining to do.'

Shelley picked up the phone again and dialled. It only rang a couple of times before it was answered.

"Hello," said Shelley, "I'd like to report a missing person."

Chapter 52.

By the time Shelley was sitting opposite a couple of police officers, she'd calmed down a little and was beginning to question whether this kind of revenge might backfire on her.

A police car outside the house would already have been noticed and Shelley would not be surprised if there hadn't been at least five text exchanges about it already. And what's more, the questions were highlighting how little she knew about her husband and that made her feel stupid.

She had told them he had left on Saturday morning to go on a business trip, a team building exercise followed by a conference in the States. She'd dropped him at the airport in time to catch his flight to Atlanta.

Yes, she'd spoken to him since. He'd called her that evening when he got to his hotel.

No, she had not called him over the weekend because he was going hiking and would not have mobile reception.

No, she didn't know which hotel he was staying at.

No, she didn't know anyone else who was with him, because it appeared there was nobody from work with him.

Yes, it was possible he was with someone else.

No, she had no idea who it might be, or if indeed he was with anyone else.

"So, when did you become concerned about your husband, Mrs Tottingham? asked the more unpleasant of the two officers, a fat balding middle-aged man who was sweating heavily even though it wasn't that warm.

"When I didn't hear from him," she replied, aware that the next question would shatter the charade of a concerned wife.

"And when was that?" asked the policeman.

"Well, I was a little concerned on Monday evening and then again on Tuesday morning, when he didn't contact me after getting back to his hotel," she said, trying to spin it in her favour.

"But you contacted us this morning?" responded the policeman, looking down at his notes as if he needed to be reminded when this morning was.

"Well, I didn't want to cause an unnecessary panic," said Shelley. "It was only when I tried to get a contact number for him from his office that I became aware that there was no trip to the States."

"So, you don't think he's gone to the States," asked the other officer, younger, probably less experienced, but certainly more empathetic than his sweaty colleague.

"I don't know where he's gone," she snapped and instantly regretted it because she didn't want both of them giving her a hard time.

"I mean, I had no reason to doubt he was going to the States until I discovered there was no organised trip. So, it's possible he went to the States, but it's also possible he flew somewhere else on Saturday morning. All I know is that I haven't heard from him since Saturday night, and I can't get through to his mobile."

"Well, it's relatively early days," said sweaty. "He could be living it up in Thailand, right as rain."

'Not helpful, and a nasty slur at the same time' thought Shelley. 'Probably where sweaty went to sweat even more'. But she decided to let his facetiousness go at this stage. She wasn't in the strongest position.

"We will make some inquires Mrs Tottingham," said the more reasonable of the officers.

They had both given her their names, but Shelley had instantly forgotten them in her haste to get them out of her house and their bloody car away from her gate. They might as well have left it with the siren on for the amount of attention it would be receiving.

"If you could inform us immediately if you hear from him, or if you think of anything else which could be helpful in tracing where he might be," he continued. "And we will be in touch if we come up with anything."

The two officers left, much to Shelley's relief. If nothing had happened to him and he was shacked up with some tart, she'd kill him herself, if not literally, certainly financially. She'd make him pay dearly for what she was going through.

Chapter 53.

It didn't take long for Shelley to lose her homicidal anger. She'd been surprised how, as time passed, she began to doubt Brian was with another woman and begin to think there had been some sort of accident.

She was sure she'd have suspected if he was seeing someone else, but then everyone thought that, didn't they? The reality was that most people didn't suspect, for longer than anyone would think.

No, what really started to bother her was that Brian was not stupid. He was a lot of things, and Shelley had called him most of them, but stupid was not one of them.

If he was with someone else, he would have kept up the pretence. He would have made sure he called when he said he would. He might have diverted his mobile to voicemail if the 'other woman' didn't know about her.

But he would have found an opportunity to call back. And, if she was going to be charitable, he did care about the girls, so calling to ask about them would have been something of a priority, even if she wasn't.

It all suggested some sort of problem, but Shelley could not begin to work out what sort of problem, or what was happening.

The next visit by the police would make that task even harder, as it simply produced more questions than answers.

Fortunately for her temper and for her privacy, the next visit was by two detectives in an unmarked car. It also suggested they were taking Brian's disappearance more seriously. How seriously, she was about to find out when they outlined to her what they'd discovered.

They had quickly established Brian had not boarded a plane to Atlanta last Saturday morning. He had not even been booked on the flight.

In fact, he had not been booked on any flight and a passport check showed he had not left the country. The airport cameras showed him leaving the cafe and heading for the exit.

A ring around the various car rental firms in the area quickly revealed a car booked in Brian's name which had been collected shortly after the security cameras showed him leaving the airport.

Ironically, this had slowed their investigation because it showed Brian's deliberate efforts to deceive his wife and it proved he was fit and well after she dropped him at the airport. This deterred the police from wading through hours of CCTV footage of the roads surrounding the airport to try to trace his journey because it was beginning to look like a domestic incident with Brian being at no risk.

They did routinely circulate the car's description and registration number to other forces, Eurostar and to all the ports where ferries operated. And that would have been the extent of their investigation unless anything more concerning turned up.

In less than 24 hours, it did. Cumbria police reported that the car had been found in a car park in the Lake District. It appeared to have been abandoned there a couple of days earlier, based on the report of a local fell walker, who had visited the same car park, three days running and had become suspicious that the same car was parked in the same position and didn't appear to have moved.

Cumbria police broke into the car, after getting confirmation from the detectives 'investigating' Brian's disappearance that it was the car they were looking for.

Inside they found a note, presumably from Brian. It described his pain at living a lie for so long, pretending to love his wife when in fact he was only truly happy when he could be his alter-ego Aston Haws, his true gay self.

In the note, Brian apologised to Shelley for this deception and asked her to explain to his girls that he loved them very much. But it concluded that he could not live that life any longer and that he had decided to take his own life.

Shelley wept at the shocking news. Cynics might assume it was because his life insurance would now be much harder to claim if an inquest did conclude Brian had taken his own life, and a suicide note was strong evidence to push a coroner in that direction.

But actually, she was genuinely upset. She was horrified at the thought of having to tell the girls what had happened and the impact of living without him hit her hard. True, that anguish would turn to anger over the next few days as she felt the humiliation that her husband was secretly gay and that their love life had been even more of a sham than she thought.

She was ashamed of what he'd done, of how he'd abandoned his daughters, and how he hadn't had the bottle to tell her to her face.

Police inquiries continued for the next few weeks as Shelley came to terms with what had apparently happened to her ex-husband, as she'd started to call him.

A fell walker responded to local appeals for information and came forward to say he'd seen Brian on Sunday morning. He said

Brian hadn't looked well, he'd given him water but he had refused his offer of help.

Mikey had also come forward because he recognised the photograph issued by Cumbria Police. He had given police the name Aston Haws which had opened up a treasure trove of gossip at that email address.

They had also traced the hotel where Brian spent his last night and found reservations at other hotels in the area. Brian's body was eventually found by police divers.

Shelley didn't care about hearing the full sordid story, nor was she bothered that Cumbria police had managed to dig up so many details surrounding Brian's suicide. But at the subsequent inquest, a new male friend, who was a lawyer, explained to Shelley that their professionalism had saved her a fortune in lost life insurance.

Brian's demeanour the previous evening, and on the morning of his death, hadn't suggested a man who was hours away from taking his own life. His secret double life and his reservations for the following days also countered the suicide theory. Together with an account of him feeling unwell, it all clouded the seemingly obvious conclusion that Brian had committed suicide, despite the note.

Clearly it wasn't enough to persuade anyone of foul play, or that somehow it was a tragic accident, but it had gone far enough to negate the suicide note to enable the coroner to record an open verdict, rather than one of suicide.

Once Shelley grasped the financial implications of this verdict, her previous sadness, shame, and even anger, had quickly turned to resentment. She would never forgive him for the deceit but she no longer had to pretend to love him and he was literally paying for it now.

Yet despite everything she'd discovered about Brian's secret life and the lies he'd told her and everyone who knew him, ending his life just wasn't like the Brian she knew.

'But then,' she concluded, 'he clearly wasn't the Brian she knew'. So, she stopped being puzzled by it.

Again, most of the evidence pointed in the same direction and when you got rid of an irritant and inherited a small fortune, you could convince yourself to ignore the evidence which did not point in the same direction.

Chapter 54.

Nigel Pye was a little early for his appointment. Nigel was always a little early. He hated being late. It was something that dated back to his school days, and the trouble you could get into if you were late. You also had little say over where you sat, or more to the point, who you sat next to if you were late.

He'd called into a small privately-run cafe near to the address of his appointment. Nigel always called in for a coffee, before every appointment, because he was always early.

It was a lovely sunny day which suited Nigel's mood. That wasn't something he could say very often. But today Nigel felt like a weight had been lifted from his shoulders, he felt like a new man, free of an invisible burden he'd been carrying around for years. In fact, he'd felt like that for a few days but more so today because he would get a chance to talk about it.

Nigel looked at his watch, still 10 minutes to wait. He decided to sit in the cafe a few more minutes and then begin the two-minute walk to his appointment.

Nigel began to think back to previous visits. Some of them had been horrible, especially in the early days. Most had been helpful, sometimes in tiny ways and sometimes his visit was the only thing that got him through the next few weeks.

There had certainly been more downs than ups, but Nigel always looked forward to his appointments. He knew they would help him and he also looked forward to seeing his old friend. But he could not remember looking forward to an appointment as much as he was looking forward to today's. He had removed the weight from his shoulders, now he would be able to get a weight off his chest.

'Funny how those two expressions were so similar but had different meanings,' he mused, as he again looked at his watch.

His reminiscing had only taken four minutes, but Nigel could not wait any longer so he got up and left the cafe for the short walk around the corner.

Two minutes later, Nigel arrived at the big townhouse, with three steps up to a central door. Nigel rang and waited for the door to be opened. He couldn't help looking at the security camera and smiling, imagining his old school friend looking at him.

'Bet the smile has surprised him' thought Nigel, as the door mechanism buzzed and the door was released. Nigel entered and went up the stairs to the first floor.

Nigel's was the last appointment of the day for Dr Geoffrey A Simpson and if Nigel was looking forward to the session Dr Simpson had been like a nervous schoolboy all day, anticipating the meeting. The pair embraced each other as Dr Simpson opened the door to his consulting room.

"Nigel, great to see you," said Dr Simpson, "And, dare I say it, you're looking really happy. I haven't seen such a big smile on your face for years."

And Dr Simpson should know. He'd been seeing Nigel professionally for five years, guiding him through countless syndromes and complexes, all of which had names equally as complicated as the symptoms they produced.

Nigel had been a mess when he'd first contacted Dr Simpson. He was severely depressed and on the brink of suicide. He had suffered what used to be called a nervous breakdown in the final year of school, and had left early without taking his A levels.

The doctors all said the blow to his head had not left him with any brain damage but all the years of bullying and stress had finally built up until Nigel had cracked up. That breakdown had spiralled downwards into deeper forms of mental health problems over the following years until Dr Simpson had effectively become Nigel's last throw of the dice.

Nigel had been to other counsellors, psychologists, psychiatrists and other 'ists' but they'd all failed to make a serious dent in his troubled existence.

One day he'd been flicking through an old diary and had seen a reference to Geoffrey Simpson, his old schoolmate, one of the few he could call a friend, although Nigel had not really had any particularly close friends.

Nigel knew him at school by his nickname, Gassy. Not that Dr Simpson could entirely blame that nickname on his school mates. His parents had to take the lion's share of the blame for that moniker. Christening someone Geoffrey Alan Simpson meant that inevitably all his possessions would be identified with the initials GAS, and schoolboy humour did the rest.

Nigel knew Gassy had trained to be a doctor and then he recalled an Old Boys newsletter had announced his specialism in psychiatry. Intrigued by the fact that the name had come back to him at such a critical time in his life, Nigel had looked up his old schoolmate on the internet.

It hadn't taken long to reveal he'd become a respected expert in dealing with depression and had a successful private practice in Reading, only an hour's drive from Nigel's home in London.

Nigel had always believed that coincidences were more than that. Everything had a purpose and there must be a reason for

Gassy's name to come back to him, especially given his relative proximity.

So, Nigel had given him a call, made an appointment, and over countless sessions, poured out the problems he was having.

The pair spent hours talking, tracing memories, finding the root cause of Nigel's problems, reliving traumas from Nigel's school days, some of which his schoolmate recalled, some other horrors were new to him and had remained unspoken for years.

Dr Simpson certainly went beyond the call of duty to support and comfort Nigel as he tried to deal with the damage caused in those Victorian school buildings all those years before.

"I'm not sure I've ever had such a big smile on my face," replied Nigel, as he pulled away from his friend and went to sit in the patient's chair.

"So, what's causing such a good mood?" asked Dr Simpson, himself unable to hide a smile.

"I just feel relief," said Nigel. "Like everything that I used to worry about is gone. All the problems in my head have been removed. Gone. Dead."

Dr Simpson smiled again.

"And how has this come about?" he asked.

"Well, you know we've talked in the past about how many strange events have happened over the past year."

Dr Simpson nodded.

"And how all of those events have ended in bad news for those who made my life such a misery at school. First, Stevenson died in that weird diving accident in Thailand, then Nicho's factory burned down and he ended up having a heart attack, then Collins topped himself, and just last week, old Burns was sentenced for sex offences."

Nigel paused.

"Go on," encouraged Dr Simpson.

"Well, I guess that one is not really that great, or part of the same series," he continued. "I mean Burns certainly was a knob but he didn't cause me any problems. Not like the others. He wasn't part of the gang. In fact, he took some stick himself, just nowhere near as much as I did. But then I guess nobody took as much as I did."

The smile now faded from Nigel's face and he went silent again.

"So, if it's not Burn's conviction, what has caused your happiness?" asked Dr Simpson, keen to get Nigel away from brooding on the fate of Rupert Burns or the ordeals he'd undergone at school.

Nigel brightened again.

"Haven't you heard?" he said. "I thought you'd know. You always seem to be more up on school gossip than I am."

"Depends what you're referring to," said Dr Simpson, a faint smile playing at the corners of his mouth.

"Tottie," said Nigel. "He's dead. Another suicide. The ringleader. The Anti-Christ. The cause of all my problems. Dead. And to think, ever since I left school, I've been the one contemplating ending it all, when all along he must have been having his own problems. Problems which were so bad, he decided he couldn't live with them any more."

Nigel again fell silent as the thought of suicide briefly dulled his joy.

"Perhaps it just shows that even in death they all had more bottle than me," he added. "I wanted to do it so many times. I just couldn't. I didn't have the strength to actually do it."

Dr Simpson stepped in quickly to stop the euphoria fading completely.

"No, Nigel, you managed to find the courage to fight on," he said.

"Sometimes it takes a lot of guts to fight for a life you've almost given up on. Fight to continue surviving in a world you despise and to keep living when you feel you no longer have a purpose or a desire to last another day."

"Perhaps," said Nigel. "I have come so close to suicide on so many occasions but he ended up the one who couldn't hack it. He was the one who couldn't cope. So, I'm still here and he's not. Well, they're not. They've all gone and I'm rid of them all forever. And I have you to thank for that."

Dr Simpson looked quizzically at Nigel. "Me? he said. "How so?"

"You helped me when nobody else could," responded Nigel. "You believed in me when nobody else did. You helped me when nobody else could. You believed in me when nobody else did. You helped me see the cause of my problems and to learn to deal with them. You gave me hope. But above all, you gave me a purpose."

Nigel continued: "And then destiny started to take over. Perhaps it was karma, or natural justice but as one by one those bastards started to disappear, I started to get better. Weird, but it was as if my life got better as theirs got worse. I became more fortunate from their misfortunes. I was getting stronger from their weaknesses. I became more alive as they died. My life became more worth living as theirs ended. It was as if their deaths were refuelling me, giving me more purpose, more power, more hope, to continue and to get better. And now with the final bastard dying, it's like I'm now fully recovered."

"You don't think it's a little strange how many tragedies have happened to the exact group that caused you so many years of misery and heartbreak?" asked Dr Simpson.

"Well, I suppose it is a coincidence," conceded Nigel.

Dr Simpson suppressed a smile, as he recalled Nigel's disbelief in coincidences.

"It is all of them," continued Nigel, smiling again. "But I guess if it was suspicious then the police would have investigated and found something. The police were presumably involved in all the things that have happened and they've never suggested there was anything untoward. All the evidence points to a bizarre set of unconnected and separate incidents which just happened to involve that group of bastards."

Nigel conceded: "I suppose there did seem to be a little doubt over Tottingham's death for a while, and the coroner didn't actually find it was suicide, but I think that was more to do with enabling the widow to claim his life insurance. Anyway, it's just a bureaucratic verdict. He topped himself, as far as I'm concerned. After all, you don't leave a note locked in your car if it's not suicide, right?"

"Yes, you've got a point there Nigel," said Dr Simpson. "So how long has this new happiness been a part of your life?"

"Well, as you know, it's been growing as my tormentors have been disappearing," said Nigel, "But it exploded when I heard the run of bad luck had finally caught up with Tottingham. That's why I changed my appointment to see you earlier. I just couldn't wait to let you know it was over. I'm convinced I'll be fine now. I feel totally different. More positive. Looking forward to life. It's as if I can start again and live the life I should have had since I was a boy."

Dr Simpson smiled again.

"Yes, I think you might be right, Nigel. You've got a new start, free of the things that were dragging you down. Go for it."

"Can I still see you from time to time?" asked Nigel. "You know, if I wobble or something."

"Of course you can," answered Dr Simpson. "And perhaps if I'm no longer seeing you professionally, we could meet up socially, from time to time."

"Yes, I'd like that," said Nigel, getting up to leave.

And on that positive note, Dr Simpson said goodbye to Nigel, and to Lemure, a name from Roman mythology which meant the malignant, restless spirits of the dead.

Dr Geoff Simpson didn't think he'd be needing that name anymore. His work was done.

About the Author:

Lloyd Watson has been a journalist for more than 40 years, working for UK newspapers, regional and national television and the international news agency Reuters.

He is now an author, Visiting Lecturer in Video Journalism at City, University of London, and runs his own media consultancy company – lloydwatson.co.uk.

He has written and published a book on video news production - *Top Tips For Making Video News*.

He lives in Hertfordshire, England.

Twitter: @lloydwatsonTV

Cover Designed by Onur Burc

Printed in Great Britain
by Amazon

Printed in Great Britain
by Amazon

74231809R00139